SPARROW'S LUNCH

SPARROW'S LUNCH

D.L. Larsen

Copyright © 2002 by D.L. Larsen.

Library of Congress Number: 2002094482
ISBN : Hardcover 1-4010-7428-6
Softcover 1-4010-7427-8

All rights reserved. No part of this book may be reproduced or transmitted in any form or by any means, electronic or mechanical, including photocopying, recording, or by any information storage and retrieval system, without permission in writing from the copyright owner.

This is a work of fiction. Names, characters, places and incidents either are the product of the author's imagination or are used fictitiously, and any resemblance to any actual persons, living or dead, events, or locales is entirely coincidental.

This book was printed in the United States of America.

To order additional copies of this book, contact:
Xlibris Corporation
1-888-795-4274
www.Xlibris.com
Orders@Xlibris.com

For my father
Donald David Dubie
1942-1998

CHAPTER ONE

There's always a because to every why in this world. Sometimes you just need to take the time to sit down and think on it to find out what it is. If I've ever learned one thing from Mr. Robbins, it's that when you're thinking on a story you need to get the history of it all good and understood before you can really get down to it. He's the only teacher that really ever got me listening to things. Sometimes, well, actually most times, I think he's the only one worth giving half of my attention to. Anyways, one thing I know is that the history of things is what's important.

So, here's the situation here. It's a doozie, but I won't bore you with too much of that extra stuff that can be annoying. Some of it you need but the other stuff, well, it will just stay other stuff. I'll just dive right in and start from where I think things get to be important.

It really starts one day when I'm walking home from another worthless day of school. I'm walking along causal, I'm sure you can picture what it is I'm talking about. It was just another walk home on another afternoon. Nothing special about it. It was right after lunch. Lunch is what usually keeps me hanging around that place considering most times I'm good and hungry and can't wait for that lunch bell to ring. I could've left a lot sooner like I do some days, not often, but some days. It would've been easy to leave especially on a nice gray day like it was. See, the thing about it is that I can shut it down in the afternoon and leave school whenever I want to. But that day, well, my stomach was extra on my case that day. There was no ifs, ands, or buts that day. I was going to have a good and tasty lunch. Period.

Besides that, Mom doesn't notice much of anything when it comes to the afternoon anyhow, least of all whatever it is that I'm doing. It makes things easy and cool. That is if what you want to do is leave school early anyways. But like I said before, I stayed around for a hot lunch. It was sloppy joe day so I had to stick around for a tasty sloppy joe. After a lunch like a sloppy joe you just need to settle in, take the afternoon off, and enjoy your full stomach. That's what I was planning on doing anyhow. There's nothing like a sloppy joe to fill you up nice.

It was a Thursday or a Friday. How I know this after some time has passed is because of the air smelling like hell. You always remember the days when the air smells like hell. It's a real pisser to things when you have to walk home and breathe in and out foul smelling air. The air smells bad every Thursday or Friday because that's the time of the week when the cattle gets slaughtered. It's not even in my own town where the cattle gets slaughtered, and the place still smells like hell. The town that does kill all the cows is like two or three towns away, and you know it like there's no tomorrow when it's a Thursday or Friday. I'm glad we stay here and not in the slaughter town. I bet there in that town you can hardly stand it.

Word is that they do all the slaughtering on Wednesday or Thursday, I'm not too sure on the particulars on that one, and then burn the blood. Who the hell thinks to burn blood for chrissakes, it smells like hell. You'd think they could come up with something different. Most times you can't smell that smell until Friday because of it having to get from the air in that town to the air in this town. You have to think about how far it has to go to get here when you think on it. Only when it's extra bad, and a big day in the cow business, does the smell get to where I live on Thursday.

But, thinking on it hard like I am, I know it must've been a Thursday and not Friday when I came across the gun. It was sloppy joe day at school. You can never forget when you had a good and tasty lunch like that. The lunch lady always knows a sloppy joe is best on a Thursday. If it was Friday it would have been pigs in a blanket with macaroni and cheese on the side. I like pigs in a blanket, too, but you can't have pigs in a blanket on a Thursday. It's sloppy joe day and that's the way it is. I remember it smelling like hell plain as day. I guess it was a bad day for the cattle in the slaughter town considering it already smelled all the way up here with it only being a Thursday.

So I'm walking along casual. I'm not taking my time like usual, but you have to keep it casual when you don't want people getting into their suspicions. People tend to get into their suspicions when they see somebody like me in the middle of the afternoon walking on the street instead of being in school like they think I should be. My steps are a little quicker, but not too much to draw any extra attention. Only on every other day of the week, besides the days it smells like hell from them burning the blood, do I take my time slow and cool. Only when the gaggers in the back of my throat aren't in overdrive and I'm not afraid of losing my good and tasty sloppy joe all over the cement. I'm never in much of a hurry to get anywhere fast, especially when my peers aren't anywhere around to try to irritate things. But when the air smells like hell, you want to get out of that air quick, so you don't take your time getting anywhere. It's fast and quick steps to get you in and out and in again. The quicker the better. But you need to keep it casual. Always keep it casual.

I'm walking along trying not to breathe in too much of the air. I'm almost home. Another clean break on another day. But before I can get anywhere other than where I happen to be walking, I see the owner of the shop, the shop that's right next door to the place where I stay, stick his grubby head out the front door of the place. It's like he was looking for me or something because when he popped his head out of the door was right when I was passing by. It's not a place where you pop your head out just for the hell of it. Things like that are too much of a coincidence to be a coincidence. He's sticking his nose into things because he wants it there. If it was somebody else I might think different about the whole thing, but it's him and I know that there's no two ways about it.

The sonofabitch, the guy who owns the shop, his name is Mike. He happens to own our crap shack, too, so I see a lot of him. And he's not the kind of guy you want to see a whole lot of. I don't know his last name. He might as well not have one as far as I'm concerned. It's just plain old Mike the sonofabitch. That's all anybody needs to know. He sure is the genuine article that guy. He's the real deal sonofabitch if there ever was one. Everybody knows he's a sonofabitch. Everybody except Mom that is. She's grateful to him because of what he's done for our family, and by family I mean Mom and me. What a stand up guy giving her a crooked job and a house for cheap and whatever else it is that he does for her. But that's Mom for you. Always grateful for crap that people like Mike the sonofabitch are giving.

I don't think Mom even knows what his last name is. She doesn't have to pay rent to him because he just takes it out of her paycheck from the shop, so there's no real reason for her to know. In fact, now that I'm thinking on it, I don't even think there's a paycheck involved when it comes to that place. I'm guessing it's cash only, under the table, or the counter as it is in this case, and Mom gets her cut at the end of every month. His name might as well be Mike Jesus Christ as far as she's concerned. Everything that joker says is like gospel to Mom. On occasion I'll call him sonofabitch to his face just to get a rise out of Mom. I can do that sometimes, and it doesn't even bother me. She's always on my case about something.

Anyways, he's waving at me right out the front door of the shop like he's my dumb dad. You can tell that he wishes like there's no tomorrow that he was my dad. It's not that he thinks I'm just one hell of a kid and wants me in his life because of me. It's all because of Mom. That guy can't stand that I'm the one thing that he can't say Mom owes all to him. He'd be my dad in a heartbeat, and be happy as a pig in a pile of crap if I'd just play along with how his head works on these things. Let me tell you something, he's not my dad and I don't want him to be. Thank God for taking care of the little things in life. It makes things much easier knowing that I don't owe that sonofabitch a thing. Mom might think she does, but I sure as hell don't.

    I can hardly move a muscle to return his gesture that I'm sure he considers is nice. He doesn't do a whole lot of things that are nice so he's not good at it. You can tell he's trying hard right now with his wagging his arms around like that. It's painful to watch and I want to ignore him like nobody's business, but I have to do something because of you can't lose your manners even if it is Mike the sonofabitch. It doesn't even cross my mind to tell him to go to hell and then spit on his parking lot. Instead I lift my fingers up a little and wiggle them so the sonofabitch will see but nobody else will. It's bad enough living with the fact that I have to know that I know the guy, but having to own up to my knowing him is a whole other thing. It's worse owning up to it. Much worse. But there's not much I can do to avoid it right at this minute.

    I think he catches the point because he sucks his filthy head back into the shop where it belongs. The one thing I can say for Mike the sonofabitch right now is that he doesn't keep at me when he can tell I'm not interested in having any kind of heart-to-heart right at this minute. I never am with him but you know what I'm saying. This might be a first for him. But then again I'm probably just giving him credit he doesn't deserve. He probably had some sort of shop emergency that couldn't wait. It has nothing to do with me. The jokers that go into that place can be awful edgy if they don't get whatever the hell it is they want when they want it. Believe me, I know what I'm saying on this one. Or maybe he just all of a sudden remembers that you don't ever stick your head out the front door of the shop. You never know who might be looking.

    But I'm glad he doesn't continue to bug me whatever the reason is anyhow before he realizes the time and thinks he needs to ride me about leaving school early. He's tried to do it before. It's not like he has any room to talk. I don't want him to even wave at me much less ride me about things that aren't his business. And there's nothing about things involving me that are his business no matter how much he and Mom try to make it that way. And like I said before, thank God for Mike the sonofabitch not being my dad.

He is a sonofabitch though. So when I say it, I'm telling the truth. What kind of guy sells the kinds of things he does for a living. He walks around like he's cool, but he's actually a sleazeball. He does things like keeping his crap-brown hair kind of long so he has to tip his head back to look at you. It's annoying when he does that. It sets things off on the wrong foot good and quick when he tips his head back to look at you. Who wants to tip their head back just to look at somebody. I don't, and I'm willing to bet my shirt that nobody else in their right mind does either. I wish he'd lose his whole head of hair. That would teach him not to look at people in funny ways.

He smells like hell, too. He's always wearing the same pair of gray pants. Not the dark kind of gray either. They are the light kind of gray that show stains and crap plain as day. You have to wonder if the guy notices how greasy and filthy his pants are. And if he does notice, you have to wonder what it is that make him think it's OK to walk around like that. I guess it doesn't bother him though. If it bothered him he'd try to change it. At least that's the way you'd think things would be anyways. He changes his shirt sometimes, well, the color of his shirt would be a better way to put it, but he's always wearing the same pair of pants. They smell like hell.

I wear the same jeans most times. I have two pairs but the one pair, well, the one pair are so tight you can see all of my business. Who wants to wear pants so tight you can see all their business. I don't, so I stick to the one pair that keeps my business my business. So, like I said before, I wear the same pair of pants every day just like Mike the sonofabitch, but the difference is I don't smell like hell. Well, not my pants anyways. My feet are a whole different thing. They get sweaty and start to smell like I have what the hell I don't know what of growing between my toes. They start to smell fast and bad. It works to my advantage though when I don't want people irritating me. It keeps them away nice. They only smell when I take my shoes off though. When they're on there's no smell. I have a good sniffer so I would know. But Mike the sonofabitch, I don't think he knows he smells like hell. He's always wanting people close, you know hugging them or talking right direct line-of-fire into their face, and you don't want people close when you know parts of you smell like hell.

Enough about him. I'm starting to get a headache just thinking on him. But that's the thing about Mike the sonofabitch. If he pokes his head into things, even if it is just for a second, it takes a good long while to shake thinking on him. So I keep walking the few steps past the shop hoping like hell Mike the sonofabitch doesn't pop his head out again, and just like that I see it. Bam, there it is. The gun is just there plain as day. I see this gun in my yard, and I get all excited. When you're walking right along and you're going out of your head because Mike the sonofabitch, and the crappy person that he is, is something you have to deal with day in and day out, it's like a miracle when suddenly you see a gun just waiting for you in your yard. Things don't seem so bad then.

I don't know if you'd call the front of where I stay a yard really with it having a lot of weeds and trash, but it's supposed to be a yard so that's what I'll call it. Good old Mike the sonofabitch will mow the lawn in front once in a while with one of those mowers without a motor. Other than that the grass, well, Mom calls it grass anyhow, gets tall and bushy and looks like anything but grass. You can't worry about the outside much though considering we live in the bad part of town and it's supposed to look like hell. Most times I don't let it bug me because of if I think on it too much my nerves get shot. I hate it when my nerves get shot.

Anyways, a minute ago I was just walking along keeping to myself like I do, trying like hell to avoid breathing through my nose and trying like hell to avoid Mike the sonofabitch, and just like that I see it. It's buried good in all the leaves, but for some reason it catches my attention. And God bless America for that. The sun just seems to shine right on it, and the thing about it is it was a cloudy foggy day, and the sun hadn't come out all day until right at that minute.

My eyes aren't so good so I'm surprised I see the thing in the leaves in the first place even with the help of the sun. Mom took me to the eye doctor once because of my teacher in the second grade riding her to do it. I couldn't see the chalkboard so my teacher got worried. The doctor said I have one eye that sees close and one that sees far and that I need glasses or else school will keep being hard. Mom said that she was a good mother and that her kid didn't need glasses, only crazies need glasses, so we left the eye doctor's office. We just left and the eye doctor was standing there like he was holding his pecker in his hand. I felt sorry for the guy. He was just doing his job, right. I would have hated glasses anyways. Besides, I've gotten used to my eyes. And the way I see things for that matter.

Most times all I see are my shoes anyhow. I concentrate on them considering nobody irritates you when you're looking down at your own shoes. When you look somebody straight into their face, it's all over. So you have two choices, pack it in and look at your shoes, or look somebody straight in the face and get down to it. Simple as that. Besides that, shoes are always the same. There aren't any of those changes or surprises that can annoy you. Like these pair here, I've only had them for a couple of months, but I already know them good. Mom had to break down and use some of her slutty money to buy me a new pair. It makes her mad when she has to spend her money on things like shoes. Especially shoes for me.

Most times she puts just about every dime she makes into buying lottery tickets. She's always waiting to hit the big one. Who the hell spends all their money, even if it is slutty money, on lottery tickets. She says she does it for me. She says, doesn't everybody want to be rich. But that's Mom for you. Always full of real big plans. I guess if I think on things, it's better that she's going to the gas station just up from where we stay to get the worthless lottery tickets instead of the beer in the bottles with caps you had to get off with a bottle opener. She hated the twist off ones, so it was always the kind you had to get open with a bottle opener. Life was full of all kinds of ugly when Mom was into her beer. But one day, all of a sudden, instead of bringing home the beer like she did everyday, before or after work it never really mattered to Mom, she brought home a fistful of lottery tickets. I still can't figure on what it was that brought about the switch, but when your mom gets off the whole beer thing you don't ask questions. You just sit back and enjoy your good fortune.

Anyways, the duct tape that was holding the other shoes together got wore out. It just wasn't holding my feet in there anymore. My feet are growing fast so I know I just grew out of them, but with Mom it's best to blame it on the duct tape. That way she doesn't ride you so much. The new shoes are white and blue running shoes. I got running shoes this time considering I might have an occasion to run one of these days, and I thought they'd be useful. I learned a lot about how things work when I was a freshman, and now that I'm a sophomore I have it good and in my head how things go. And things like running shoes will be useful. Now with my new shoes getting broken in the way I like them and my finding the gun, well, it's a match made in heaven.

CHAPTER TWO

It's not such a weird thing that I find a gun in my yard considering my neighborhood. It's crappy and this situation here doesn't surprise me one bit. I guess it's not all that fair to say it's a neighborhood considering the house where Mom and me stay is the only house for a few blocks, so it's not a real neighborhood like you'd think. My block is a small block, but things tend to happen. If people want to get into something, they come here to do it. It's not a real neighborhood so people don't treat it like it is. It's where I live, but that doesn't seem to matter to anybody but me. When people want to get into something there's no sense in them doing things anywhere where it might mess up a regular part of town. We stayed in the good neighborhood for a while, so I know what it is I'm talking about. Nothing ever happened there. I was nice and cozy. We stayed in one of those big old houses by the park that just smell rich. But I'll get into that later.

I grew up in the same house we stay in now. Right along the busiest street in town. It's the kind of street where everybody that wants to get somewhere important has to take it. All sorts ride up and down this street at all times of day. Some of the cars are super-nice to look at so you don't mind it so much, but the most of them I could do without. Mom and me lived in that nice place for a while, but moved right back in here. Some people just aren't meant to stay in a nice place for long. So it's back to Mom and me in the same crap shack as always.

Next door on the one side of where we stay is the shop, and on the other side is a place where there used to be a house, but it was torn down long before I ever came into things. Some of the wood of the torn down house is still there though. When it rains or snows and the pile of wood gets wet, it smells good and rotten. It's old wood anyways so it smells old all on its own from time to time, but when it gets wet that's a whole different thing. I guess they haven't had the time to pick the wood up yet. In life there's just priorities for things and that's obviously not one of them. They should have torn down my crap shack at the same time as the house next door. That place couldn't have been in much worse shape than where we stay. I can't imagine how Mike the sonofabitch pulled that one off.

And the shop is a nasty place. What a thing to have to live next door to. You haven't seen anything until your house sits side by side with a shop like that. There is something wrong with people who go in the place, and these are the kinds of people you have to deal with when you are in the situation I'm in. I would ask them what's wrong with them going into a place like that, but you can't really understand a thing when it comes to anything they're talking about, so it's pointless. Not that I could really give a crap anyways, but sometimes you do wonder on these things.

Not a one of them walks out the front door of the shop either. You could be walking by at any time of the day or night and you'd think the place is going belly up at any second considering it looks deserted. You can see the lights on through some of the windows at night, but you never see a soul go into the place. Not even Mike the sonofabitch. But I know exactly who it is that goes in, and I know exactly who it is that comes out. When you live next door to a place like that, and you sit on the front porch when you want to get out but have no place to go, you know how it is that things work, and you know who it is that's doing them.

They go in the back door. It's convenient to use the back door because of there being an alley back there and not a whole lot of traffic. They go in the back door secret, and come out the same way. Sometimes they'll walk between my house and the shop and try pretending like they've been walking along the street casual all along. And when I'm sitting on my front porch, minding my own business like you learn to do, they always try to strike up a conversation. No matter how it is that I don't look at them and don't give a damn what they are saying, I can never seem to get out of it. I just have to sit there and listen to whatever the hell it is they are trying to say. I sit there and listen considering you can't lose your manners even when you want to with the jokers that stumble in and out of that place with what the hell I don't know what kind of look in their eyes. I guess sometimes it's better not to even think on those things. It's hard enough to have to listen to what the hell it is that they are trying to say with their fuzzy-fat tongues filling up their filthy mouths that said who knows what to Mom. I've seen all sorts when it comes to the shop.

For reasons that are probably pretty obvious already, I don't like to spend a lot of time where we stay. Most times I try not to if I can avoid it. It's depressing staying at home when you don't have nice stuff around or when you have a mom that's on your case all the time or when you're trying to avoid most everybody that's trying to come into your life. I don't do much. I get by. That's what I do. I get by. Regular people don't know what that's like, but I do. I have a feeling Mom agrees with me considering we're both rough trade, but she tries hard to play like she's worth something. Like with the lottery tickets. I know she wants to strike it rich so we can get a nice house by the park. We both know what a house by the park is like, and we sure as hell both know it's better than where we are right now. But the town we live in either you're worth something or you're not. It's easy to tell the difference around here.

Before you get the wrong idea though, let me tell you something. My town is an upstanding place. Where we live is this place called Fort Harmony, Colorado. I'd be proud to be from here if Mom and me weren't rough trade like we are. It's a clean place, and the people are nice enough if they don't get into their suspicions. It's tough to find one that doesn't, but that's a whole other thing. It's a real thing of beauty around here. The trees are tall and things are green, when it's not winter, of course. It smells good most times. That is when it's not a Thursday or a Friday like I was telling you about before. Even the snow around here smells good. It makes you not mind the walk to and from school and wherever else you need to go when it's cold outside. I like all times of the year in Fort Harmony. But, like I said before, it's hard to enjoy it when people are always getting into their suspicions and not letting you be.

Fort Harmony sure is far from Boston though. But that's Mom for you. She's always trying to forget things like leaving Boston and everything behind, and ending up in Fort Harmony. She just got on a bus one day and rode it across country until she just couldn't stand riding the thing anymore. Her stomach got upset from riding and looking out the window when she finally said enough is enough. This is as far as she got to. Good old Fort Harmony, Colorado. She swears she could have been a big and famous actress in Hollywood if she ever would have made it there. That's where her real big plans were taking her in the first place. But that's when I came into things and made it hard to do just about anything. It's no secret Mom didn't want me, I'm no fool, but what I can't figure on is why she didn't take care of it. I know you know what it is I'm talking about. I don't ask her these things though because of her getting upset when I try to get into her business. Besides, nobody wants to see the way Mom carries on when she runs for her box of tissues and rosary beads whenever it is that she happens to be upset. Nobody wants to see that.

I think Mom could've been somebody if she wasn't interested in the wrong things. Parts of me can't help but think things could be different for me and Mom. It's hard to get those kinds of things out of your head once they're in there. The kind of person Mom is, well, I guess things could go either way on that one. People like Mom can do things nobody else can. I guess things are up to her on how to use them and not me which is a damn shame. Mom knows how to mess up things other people would know not to. Like where we stay isn't fit for anybody, but she seems happy being right where we are. At least she doesn't do a thing to change it, well, anything besides the lottery tickets that is. The way Mom is I can know that we're here for the long haul. Some things are just too hard to get up off the couch and change.

Maybe she was worth something back in Boston, but who knows. People usually don't leave things that are working out good for them. You never really know anything for sure when it comes to Mom, and she sure as hell isn't going to tell you anything. Sometimes she tries hard to make a go of things here. Like when she talks about reading books and things like that. I guess she figures regular people read books so she should, too. It's not like she knows anybody around here who would even care about that stuff anyhow, and it's not like she'd ever even like to be a regular kind of a person. But these are the things I'm talking about. It's always a big contradiction when it comes to Mom.

Boston doesn't sound so bad. I've never been there so I can't say much about it from a personal perspective. And Mom sure as hell is tight-lipped about the place so she's no use. I've never been anywhere outside of Fort Harmony, so this is really it for me as far as knowing things goes. Anyways, Mom left Boston because of her family. She says they're mean and nasty. That's all she ever says about them, that they were mean and nasty. She said the weather was bad, too. It was humid and made her hair frizzy. That's the word she used, too, frizzy. But I can't think things were much worse considering how we live in the bad part of town even if her hair was frizzy. But right now I don't want to think on Mom's hair. I don't want to think on Mom at all as a matter of fact. Right now I need to focus all my attention on the gun, and like I told you about before, I'm all excited.

CHAPTER THREE

So I'm stopped quick right in my tracks between the shop and where I stay, but I keep it quiet. My head is going so fast I get dizzy and think I'm going to fall over. But I talk myself out of it considering you have to keep a clear head in these situations. The last thing you can do is get dizzy and lose your marbles over something that is the best thing that's ever happened to you. So I spread my legs a little to stop myself from tipping over. I breathe in through my nose deep even though that's the last thing I want to do with the air smelling like hell. But you need to weigh your options with things. Right now I can see plain as day that if I wasn't to breathe the foul air in through my nose and out through my mouth I'd draw a lot of attention that I don't need right at this minute. When the people around here see something like a guy laid out flat on the sidewalk all because of he lost his marbles from being dizzy, well, they get good and into their suspicions then. I think I'm good for now though.

I know Mom is home because of I can see out of the corner of my eye the front door being wide open. I know she's home but I know she's passed out. She's always passed out at this time of day. And when Mom is asleep, like I know she's good and asleep right now, there's not a thing in the world that could wake her up. I guess she's just used to the noise that comes along the street. Me, well, I don't think I'll ever be used to all the noise. Especially not when I'm trying to catch some zs. But Mom doesn't notice a thing. Her sleep is her sleep, and there's no messing with it. She wouldn't hear if I was yelling my lungs out much less if I was to root through the leaves, but I like to play it safe and keep it quiet. Just in case. Mom's been known to pull a fast one or two.

The gun looks old and rusty and not worth much. Well, I tell myself, it's not worth much if you don't know how to look at it. You have to look past the obvious things about it and see the prospects. It'll do just fine. It's mine now and it's a thing of beauty. My stomach gets these tingly feelings at all the prospects that can come my way now. I'm not so smart but you don't need to be so smart these days to get around. What you need are prospects. And, well, now for the first time I have them. They're laying smack-dab right in front of my face. It sure is a thing of beauty though. It's just laying there in the leaves like it fell out of the trees. It's like it fell out of the trees right along with the rest of the leaves that have turned all sorts of colors and fallen off like they're supposed to do this time of year. It's like it was an act of Mother Nature for chrissakes. And it's all for me. Beautiful.

For about a second I wonder where it came from and who it belongs to. Only for a second though. Like I told you before, my house is next door to the shop so the possibilities are endless. The last thing you need is one of these jokers thinking you took something that belongs to them, and have them come after you to get it back. I wish you could see the jokers that go in and out of this place. Then you'd know what it is I'm talking about. There's no telling what they might think much less the things they might do.

So, instead of sitting here with my thumb up my ass thinking about who it might belong to, I walk over and pick the thing up. It takes a lot out of me to pick my feet up from where I'm standing and keep it steady to walk the couple of feet I need to get at it. It's hard, but I do good. I even manage to keep it a little cool so it doesn't look like I'm up to anything. I don't need to draw any attention to myself. I hold it for a while and feel what I'm sure those jokers feel when they go into the shop. Not that I think I'm anything like those jokers. All I'm saying is it gets your blood pumping. That's all. And right now my blood is pumping good and fast.

My life so far has been a crap shoot. I'm pretty sure you could tell by now. Well, I guess it's been a crap shoot until now with the gun. Now I can see a definite line in my life of before and after. This is the first lucky thing that's happened to me. I've never been the type to find a dollar on the street so I could get an extra milk at lunch. Not that I need extra money for milk most times because of the lunch lady being nice and giving me extra just because. And something like finding a cigarette butt that's only half gone so I could smoke the rest has never happened to me. All the ones I find around here are always smoked right down to the nub. Not that I smoke or anything. It's disgusting and smells like hell, but I sure would look cool and tough with a butt in my hand. But I've never been that guy, well, until now like I told you before. I'm one lucky bastard finding this thing in my own yard.

Cars keep driving by behind me and all I want is a moment to myself. I'm shaky enough as it is. Most times there's not a whole lot of cars this time of day considering it's right in the middle of the day, so it makes them extra noticeable. Especially since right now I wish everybody in the whole town would just get the hell out of here. Well, I wish they would get the hell out of here just because, but today I want them out of here like nobody's business. This is a momentous occasion. Things like this just don't happen every day of your life. All I want is the time to acknowledge it with a little peace and goddamn quiet so my nerves don't get shot. But the cars keep coming, interrupting my momentous occasion, all because of my living on the busiest street in town. Who the hell picks to live on a street like this anyhow.

We stay right across from the college of all places. It's nice enough to look at with the buildings and trees, but it's the people that ruin it. Not that the people on my side of the street are doing such a bang-up job either, but at least they notice that you are the hell around even when you don't want them to. Like with the jokers I was telling you about before. The people at the college, well, it's a whole different thing. Sometimes those college kids have an attitude when it comes to things. Like they are the only ones in the world worth a damn. Maybe they are. Who knows.

All I know right now is that I want a minute alone to think. I need a minute to think. I know the prospects are endless, but I can't think. All that damn noise. I want to yell and tell everything to shut the hell up, but I think better of things. If I was to yell I might get the attention of Mike the sonofabitch, or even worse, I might wake Mom up off the couch to see what it is I'm yelling about. The last thing you want to do is see the kind of ugly that comes when you wake Mom up and she has to get up off the couch. I know what it's like, so I get a hold of myself and keep the hell quiet.

Then, just like I sneezed all over myself or something, I get a horrible thought in my head. What if one of those cars saw me pick it up from the ground. I'd be screwed then. I can't remember how it was exactly that I picked it up either. Like, did I do it slow and cool like I was picking up a penny or something, or did I fumble around like an idiot with my ass in the air for too long. How can you not remember what it was that happened two minutes ago. I hate it when I don't know if I have a need to worry. What I do know though is that I'm holding the gun plain as day right now, so I guess things like how it got there are besides the point. I sure wish I could remember though. Things like this kill me.

And whether or not did I have my ass sticking straight up in the air for too long, well, that's not really something to worry on right now. It's kind of hard not to notice me anyways with all this blonde hair. So I know they see me even if they don't mean to. It's the scary kind of blonde. Albino-like. It's ridiculously noticeable especially on a day like today when it's good and gray outside. My head looks like a stupid light bulb or something. So I shove the thing in my pocket smooth instead of standing here with all these cars like I'm holding my pecker in my hand. Sometimes you just have to know when to wisen the hell up.

It slides in my coat pocket nice and cool. I look around to see if anybody's watching, but I'm clean. It's a thing of beauty how it just slides in my pocket like it belongs there. I tell myself those college kids couldn't give a damn about what the hell I'm doing even if they saw me anyways. I know that for a fact. And Mike the sonofabitch, well, if he wanted to get into things he would've done it long before now. That's one thing about Mike the sonofabitch. He's predictable so there's not much he can do to sneak up on things. But then again, I don't want to test my luck with him today. Leave it to him to change his ways on me today.

So I go into the house through the door that's probably been open all afternoon. I'm walking with this gun in my pocket and I try to keep things quiet and still. I don't shut the door behind me because what's the point. All those jokers that go to the shop won't see anything new if they come in and see Mom spread-eagle on the couch anyhow. It's not like they haven't seen it before. Besides, I have other business to attend to like thinking of the prospects. My nerves got shot because of all those cars making it hard to think. I need to settle myself down. I hate it when my nerves get shot. I tried like hell to avoid it. I guess some things you can't avoid though. There are so many cars and it's the middle of the day for chrissakes. There are so many stupid prospects and my mind's a useless blank.

CHAPTER FOUR

Before I go any further telling you more about my situation making you think I'm some kind of weirdo or something, I think I should give myself a formal introduction. My name is Dusty Sparrow. No kidding. That's my name and I think I don't have any friends because of it. Maybe I don't have any friends for a lot of reasons, but my name seems to be the most obvious one I can come up with. I have been doomed since birth with a name like that, and Mom is too preoccupied to know it. Her real last name isn't even Sparrow, it's O'Malley, but it changed since she moved out here from Boston to make a new life for herself. And if I might say so myself, Bravo, Mom. Bang-up job. I guess Mom's the type of person who thinks you can change things by changing your name. Mom has a lot of things in her head about life that just don't add up for me, and changing an upstanding name like O'Malley to Sparrow is one of them.

Anyways, I think she got the idea for using Sparrow for a name from a book. I think that's the way the story goes. I heard her telling it to somebody once at the shop, but I can't be too sure about it considering I was eavesdropping. You have to know if you're eavesdropping you might not get the whole story. It's a good way to learn things, but you have to take it with a grain of salt. I would've asked her right then and there myself if I wouldn't have messed things up for her good. When your kid isn't supposed to be around, the last thing you need for him to do is pop his head up and start asking questions. Things can go all kinds of crazy when something like that happens. When you're there in secret, you need to stay there in secret. So I thought better of things. Now I just have to live with half the story in my head. I guess I should be happy that I at least know half, but it makes me crazy when I have to make up the other half myself. Your head can take you all kinds of places on that one.

Hell, I wouldn't even know about her real last name being O'Malley if I hadn't gotten a hold of some old mail addressed to Mom with O'Malley written right on it. I wanted to ask her about it right then and there when I found it, but you can't ask your mom about something you found when you were looking somewhere you shouldn't have been looking. So I didn't bring it up then and I don't bring it up now and I'll probably never bring it up all because of I'm sure there will never be a time for it. There's never much time for things when it comes to Mom. And besides, I'd rather not see the kind of look Mom would get on her face if the secret she thought she kept good and under wraps all these years wasn't such a secret after all. I'll be good and far away before I even think of mentioning it. And I plan on mentioning it. Someday anyways.

But when I was eavesdropping I heard her say something about sparrows being some kind of messenger between man and God. You should've heard her, too. She was talking like she's so smart and has read every dumb book that was ever written. I don't know who she thinks she might impress. I know she didn't know a thing about the person she was talking to about the whole name thing. I was eavesdropping, but you know when a voice is a strange one. She'll tell a perfect nobody in her life all kinds of things, but she keeps it all under wraps when it comes to me. And other than the perfect nobodies she tries hard to impress, the only person she sees on a regular basis is Mike the sonofabitch, and she just has to show the hell up and that does it for him. He could really give a crap about the whole book thing anyhow. I'm sure whoever it was that she was talking to couldn't give a crap either. But she tries hard.

A messenger for chrissakes. She'll say whatever it is she has to though. She's always concerned about getting into heaven one way or the other, and if talking about a worthless book gets her there, well, she'll do what it takes. I don't know when she's ever read a book. I've never seen it before. Knowing Mom she watched the TV movie and passed it off as reading. What a place to get an idea for a name anyways. A dumb book she probably never read. But that's Mom for you. And as far as Dusty goes, well, I don't know where that came from. Who the hell thinks up a name like Dusty for chrissakes. It doesn't even sound good. Your guess is as good as mine on that one.

And first of all, I don't know why any judge would let anybody, especially somebody like Mom that doesn't really know what the hell life is all about, change an upstanding name like O'Malley to something like Sparrow. I know for a fact Mom had to talk to a judge to make everything good and legal. I haven't found the papers to prove it yet, but I'm looking. A judge is called a judge because of them being able to tell what is good and what is bad. But knowing how Mom is, if that judge was a man, and I know it had to be a man, it couldn't have been very hard to persuade him into letting her do such a dumb thing. A lot of guys get a cloudy head when it comes to Mom. It's just one of those things that happens in this world.

I'm not even going to mention the nurse who filled out my birth certificate. Now I know that nurse was a lady. Most nurses are so I'm figuring the one who wrote my birth certificate was. Why the hell would a nurse with a stand-up job let Mom name me Dusty in the first place and Sparrow along with that. She had to notice that it's a name that will doom the poor baby before it even gets a fair shake out of life. The only thing I can possibly think up on that one is maybe she was told she couldn't say anything about a new baby's name, and that her job was just to write down whatever the hell the mom was saying even if it's the most senseless thing you've ever heard. But besides my thinking on it, I'm willing to bet she was no fool, so it keeps at me how she could let a little tiny baby who just came into things, and hasn't done a damn thing to anybody yet, leave the hospital with a piece of paper that says his name is Dusty Sparrow. Things just don't add up in my head on that one even if my suspicions on the whole thing are correct. You have your name for your whole life, so I just wish that somebody, especially that nurse, would have the balls to say to Mom that enough is enough. But not many people can do that when it comes to Mom.

It wasn't always just supposed to be Mom and me. Another little baby was supposed to come into things when I was about eight or so. I thought Mom was getting fat so I asked her, I said, Mom why are you getting so fat. I said it just like that, too, considering when you're eight you don't know any better. I knew things were different though because of she didn't ride me like she usually does. You don't just call your mom fat and not have her ride you. She's always concerned about the whole weight thing, so when I think back on it I can't believe I said something like that to her.

But she smiled big and sat me down for the first and last heart-to-heart we ever had. She said that a new little baby was going to come into things. I said OK and went into my room and thought about things a new little baby needs to know. I knew even back then that there's just things a new little baby needs to know about so they don't get scared. You have to tell them how things really stand, especially in the bad part of town, even if they don't want to hear it. They need to know because of things being the way they are, and staying the way they are for that matter. It's not pretty, but it's better to know than to be left the hell in the dark. I wish I had somebody around to tell me the way of things before I had to figure them out all on my own. But I didn't so that's just the way it is.

I thought about the things I was going to tell the new little baby everyday. Well, everyday until Mom cried hard in the bathroom and got bloody and then all of a sudden she wasn't so fat after that. I know now that she lost the baby. I don't mean lost like a bag of groceries, but like, well, you know what it is I'm trying to say. Anyways, it took me a while to figure that one out. She never told me, but I knew things were different considering she went for the box of tissues under the kitchen sink just about every worthless minute after being bloody in the bathroom. I'm not even going to mention about the rosary beads.

She seemed happy while she was fat. Mike the sonofabitch seemed extra happy about the whole thing, too. You can do your own math on that one. Then, all of a sudden, it was right back to the couch. The bathroom stayed bloody like that for a while. I didn't say anything about it all because of those aren't the kinds of things you mention to Mom. She just couldn't seem to get up off that couch for weeks, but when you're eight those weeks seem like years. There was no feeding herself much less cleaning up the mess in the bathroom. I tried to stay away from it as much as possible, but when it's the only bathroom in the house, you have to do what you have to do.

I never asked about it because of my knowing it wasn't a good thing to ask your mom what happened to the new little baby that was supposed to come into things. It must have been nature or something that knew she's not worth a damn as a mom. You always hear about how those things happen in nature. Sometimes I'm glad there's no little baby, but most times I want one bad. Mom may not be worth a damn as a mom, but I'd be a good brother. I'd try at least. I had everything down that I wanted to say and how I wanted to say it. Everything the new little baby needed to know was everything I was ready to tell it. When I think of that nurse who let Mom take me out of the hospital with a name like mine, well, it makes me sort of glad it's just Mom and me even though it wasn't always supposed to be just that way.

But never mind all that. Back to my name. Ever since I first started school my so-called peers make these cawing noises every time I walk by, you know like a stupid bird or something. The cafeteria at school is the worst. All day my peers play like they're upstanding and just plain noble. They keep it cool in front of the teachers and anybody else who might give a damn. Especially around Mr. Robbins. Now there's a stand-up guy for you. Nobody would ever give you a hard time when Mr. Robbins is hanging around. Even if he's minding his own business and not paying attention to what the hell is going on around him, nobody's going to say anything. I don't know what makes things like they are. It's just the way they happen to be when it comes to Mr. Robbins. He's a stand-up guy. He really gives a goddamn when it comes to things.

But back to my original point about my so-called peers. The cafeteria with them is the worst. Most times I'm clean and not up to a thing, but my peers feel the need to irritate me because of my situation. Who likes to go to school and listen to Brian Farrell get into it about Mom or make those stupid cawing noises because of my name. Who needs to know my business. It's my business. It's nobody else's business. My business is my business.

Besides that, my name isn't the only one that's so bad in school. What about Candy Carmichael. Who has a name like Candy Carmichael for chrissakes. She has all sorts of friends. Nobody irritates her in the cafeteria. Nobody seems to give one measly thought to the fact that her name is on the weird side of things. Maybe it's because of her smelling good. I don't know how to say exactly how she smells, but I just know it's nice. I know it's not perfume or any of those things that get stuck up your nose and make it hard to breathe. I know it's not that. Sometimes I find myself thinking about the way Candy Carmichael smells even when I'm not sitting behind her in Mr. Robbins's class. But she has all sorts of friends that Candy Carmichael. She's even said hey to me before. So as far as I go, I think she's OK.

There's not much I can do about the cawing, but I can keep my peers away from me if I want to in the cafeteria. It's easy if I take the time to concentrate on the situation at hand. All I have to do is take off my shoes. They leave quick because of my feet smelling bad and rotten. Sometimes I can't even stand the smell myself, but it keeps my peers from irritating me. Especially that stupid Brian Farrell. He's a pansy when it comes down to it. A dainty one that guy. But it smells like hell when I do that. Even when it comes to my sort of new white and blue running shoes. They already smell bad, and it's only been a couple of months. It doesn't take long for you to get that smell in your shoes if you want it there. But I go to the cafeteria to eat my lunch, not to put up with my stupid peers, so I do what I have to do.

Most times I avoid my peers at all costs. Like I hardly know what my locker looks like because of my not going there too often. Sure all my books are in there, but I don't use them, so there's not much occasion to get in my locker. I don't have any pictures taped up on the inside like most everybody else does. I can go without pictures hanging on the inside of my locker. If I was going to put something in there it would be a mirror so I could see what's going on behind my back. Anyways, I know my locker combination good though. You have to know your locker combination good these days considering your business is your business, and nobody else needs to know your locker combination even if you don't get there all that often. I threw the tag away that had it typed right on it. I tore it up good into small pieces so nobody can get into my business. I know the combination by heart. It's 25 right—15 left—4 quick right. I told you I know it.

So anyways, I don't go to my locker much because of it sometimes being worse than the cafeteria. Like this one time I was just minding my own business like I do standing in front of my locker I just opened, and some stupid funny guy comes along and slams the door closed right on my fingers. Right on my fingers like it was a hilarious thing to do. It hurt like hell, but you can't let them know it hurt like hell. Who wants to slam somebody else's fingers in their own locker unless they're trying to be funny and irritating even if they do say they're sorry like an upstanding citizen. I'm no fool though. I know what a guy means when he slams another guy's fingers in a locker.

The funny thing about it was that I didn't have any business being at my locker. I opened it and played like I needed something important because of Candy Carmichael's locker being a few rows down. She smelled super-nice in Mr. Robbins's class so I followed her down the hall so I could smell her some more. I didn't get to smell her too much that day. You remember things like that, like not getting to smell Candy Carmichael's good smell as much as you'd want to because of the guy sitting right next to you. I don't even know what the hell his name is, but whoever he is he smelled like hell that day. The guy looks just like me. You'd think we were brothers or something, so you'd think I'd know his name but I don't. But because of Mom being no chef, the kind of smell he had, well, I'd never smelled a smell like that before, but I knew as sure as I'm here that it was some kind of food. Sometimes it got stuck up my nose like that day and gets in the way of the good smell of Candy Carmichael. I get mad when I have to smell his stink of burnt food when I have Candy Carmichael right in front of me for chrissakes. You'd fall right out of your stupid socks if you could smell Candy Carmichael. It's a thing of beauty the way that Candy Carmichael smells.

So I followed her considering I didn't get my fill of her good smell. Because of my not wanting her to think I'm some kind of weirdo or something, and have her know that I was following her, I stopped at my locker and turned the combination 25 right—15 left—4 quick right. I get the thing open and then all of a sudden, not two seconds later, just like that, bam. My fingers feel like they're going to fall off right from where they were smashed from the locker door. It made me good and angry considering everybody in the whole school was laughing at me like something was so funny. Everybody except Candy Carmichael that is. I saw her standing behind whoever those people were that were laughing. She was just standing there looking at me with those sad eyes you don't see all that often. Like I told you before, she's OK as far as I go.

The funny thing is that I didn't run out of the school like I wanted to. I thought about leaving, but it came to me that I couldn't just leave even though my fingers were slammed in my locker, and even though I was angry about it. I had to stay for lunch considering it was Salisbury steak day. You always get mashed potatoes on Salisbury steak day. And I know like there's no tomorrow that the lunch lady will put an extra little bit of butter on the mashed potatoes for me. I can always count on the extra butter.

Nobody said anything in the cafeteria that day. It made the steak that much better. I'm guessing they got their fill with the locker bit. You don't notice your fingers throbbing like hell when everybody shuts the hell up and lets you eat your Salisbury steak and mashed potatoes in peace. It was a thing of beauty even though my hand ached like there's no tomorrow. There's nothing like eating Salisbury steak and mashed potatoes in peace.

CHAPTER FIVE

So, back to the gun. I walk into the house. I walk right past Mom laying spread-eagle on the couch in her usual passed-out clothes, a tank top and cut-off pink sweat pants. It doesn't surprise me a bit to find her on the couch. She's always on the couch this time of day. Who the hell buys pink sweat pants anyhow and then cuts them off into shorts when the knees wear out. I don't know who besides Mom would do something like that. Sometimes she even goes up to the gas station to buy the worthless lottery tickets in her passed-out clothes. It's amazing how sometimes she can't even take the time to look decent to walk out of the house. She's in too big a hurry to strike it rich to think about how she looks in her tank top and cut-off pink sweat pants I guess. All they do is make you look big no matter how skinny you are. She's skinny, too. It's not that. It's just that the pink sweat pants don't do a thing for her. Not that anybody notices when it comes to Mom though.

I guess skinny is the thing nowadays. You can tell this because of everybody trying to be skinny. I never really noticed it much or gave it too much of my attention up until just recently. Like the girls at school who I see during lunch eat a roll and drink a juice or something. One roll and that's it. What I can never figure on is why anybody would turn down something like sausage pizza on sausage pizza day. It's good and hot. You know it's good pizza because of the cheese never gets hard on top. Well, not on mine anyways considering I eat it fast, so I guess I can't say much about anybody else's piece of pizza. I could eat four or five pieces and not think twice about it. But even then on sausage pizza day those stupid girls stick to their plain rolls playing like it's the tastiest thing ever. Most times they're skinny anyways. It doesn't stop them from trying hard to be even skinnier though. But Mom, well, I guess that's something else she has going for her if you believe in those kinds of things. She's skinny and bony. Sometimes, like when she's asleep on the couch like she is now, you can see her ribs poking out. Who wants their ribs poking out of their shirt for chrissakes. I don't. But Mom, well, who knows about Mom.

People say Mom is pretty. I can't argue really. She has a nice face. She looks a lot like those girls on the magazine covers, you know like on those magazines Mike the sonofabitch sells. She has nice teeth when she smiles. Her hair's nice, too, all shiny. It's long and straight. It just goes from the top of her head down in the middle in all directions, but it never covers her face so everybody can get a good look. And all kinds of people want to get a good look when it comes to Mom. Her hair is the same color as mine. Ridiculous blonde. Albino-like. If I was a girl people might think we were twins because of our hair and eyes being the same color. I look just like her, but I guess the same things that work for her don't do a thing for me with my being a guy. Nobody goes out of their head when I'm around. Hell, I don't even know if many people notice when I'm standing right next to them other than to caw at me and those kinds of things. Only Mom. It's always pretty much always all about Mom.

Mike the sonofabitch says she can use those things, you know being pretty and skinny and having an accent from being from Boston, to her advantage with her working at the shop. He gave her the job forever ago, but he still says stuff like that to her and she smiles big like he just handed her a filthy crown for a beauty pageant or something. It's a terrible thing when she smiles big at the sonofabitch Mike. Even her teeth don't seem so nice when she smiles like that at people like Mike the sonofabitch. But that's Mom for you. Always smiling big at the wrong things.

I wouldn't know anything about those kinds of things though. About the jokers being the way they are and liking the things they like. And least of all Mike the sonofabitch. Who knows what that guy thinks most times anyways much less when he gets all out of breath quick every time Mom looks at him sideways. Nothing seems to do it for that guy like Mom does. And let me tell you something, Mom does that to all kinds of guys. She couldn't really give a goddamn what the hell it is that she does to them just as long as she gets the things she wants out of life. She'll smile big for just about anybody that can give her those things. And the things she wants out of life are easy cash and easy living. The usual getting by kind of thing. That's about it as far as I can figure.

Most times you see people and they have plans for things and are willing to do what it takes. Like take me. I have plans like there's no tomorrow. You can just look at my face and know there's things going on behind these eyes. It's the prospects that count. Even Mike the sonofabitch has things he wants out of life. Sure, you can hardly stomach the guy, but he has things going on in that greasy old head of his all the time even if it is only to make dirty money. He's still doing what it takes. All I can figure on for Mom is the stupid couch she never wants to get off of and the stupid lottery tickets she buys whole fistfuls of. Some days I just wish for her to get the hell up off that couch, but most days it's easier just to say to hell with it. At least I know the chances of her riding me are less when she stays on that ugly couch.

Mom works the night shift now. She sleeps all day spread-eagle on the couch like she is considering it's still the afternoon, and considering her needing her sleep for work at night. Mom didn't always work the night shift though. But she works late now because of the sonofabitch Mike told her she could make more money working the night shift. Whatever that sonofabitch says is like gospel to Mom. When I was a kid though she had to work the day shift because of my being so young. I'd go to school then to

Mom's work until after her shift was over. She was always anxious about me being alone in the house when I was a kid, so I was stuck behind the cash register counter where I couldn't make one little peep. I never understood that considering the house is right next door to where she spends the better part of her life in that dumb place making her slutty money. It's right next door for chrissakes.

When I ask her why she doesn't get a stand-up job at someplace besides the shop she says she owes it to Mike the sonofabitch to stay. Like this one time I thought Mom would be good at being a hair cutter or something else that has to do with being pretty. Her hair always looks nice even if it isn't clean most times. A hair cutter is a stand-up job. All Mom said about the subject, about being a hair cutter, was that she's seen all the lice she wants to see to last ten lifetimes. I've never seen lice before. Not in a place like Fort Harmony anyways.

So then Mom wants to know how I think you're supposed to get from here to there at one of those so-called stand-up jobs without a car. It's hard to get to where you need to go with no car. So I stopped asking because of her having a good point, with having no car. To make a long story short, it's been the shop since before I ever came into things and it's the shop still. Nothing ever changes much in the bad part of town. And Mom, well, I can see Mom on that dirty couch till her hair turns gray and falls out from the roots from something not being right in her body. But that's a ways down the road and best not to think on right now.

But I'm passing the couch confident right under her nose with the gun in my pocket like it's meant to be there. I keep a hold of it tight because of you need to always keep a hold of your good fortune. She doesn't even flip over on her side or anything, so I know she's passed out good. The last thing I need is Mom on my case right now. When I think on it, I'd bet anything she'll be out like that all afternoon considering she wasn't even home before I went to school. I'm walking confident only because I know she's good and out for a while, but I still know better than to press my luck. Like I said before, I don't even shut the door behind me and disturb things that are quiet like I want them to be.

The place smells like hell. Not only was it bad outside, but now I have to deal with it inside, too. I know it's coming from the kitchen. You can just tell when things that smell like hell are coming from the kitchen even though the whole house smells by now. Mom has never been a chef no matter what she thinks. When she tries to cook it smells like hell. We eat TV dinners before Mom goes to work from time to time even though the TV is shot most of the time. It's hard to screw those up. They're OK, but they're no sloppy joe. Sometimes I can't stomach them though. When you've eaten one too many TV dinners in your lifetime, you just get to the point where you say enough is enough and you won't eat another bite. Cafeteria food suits me just fine. I get filled up at lunch time so long as my peers don't irritate me and that Brian Farrell keeps his cheap mouth shut. The lunch lady is nice to me and gives me extras when it comes to my lunch, so most times I don't eat dinner because of Mom being no chef and my getting filled up on lunch with the lunch lady being nice. You just have to learn how to weigh your options with things.

So just to suit my curiosity on where that foul smell is coming from, I walk through the living room where Mom is passed out and into the kitchen. The place looks just as bad as always. I don't know why I ever think it might be any different. I guess I can't blame her for not cleaning the place up considering it has been crappy for a long time. Long before we ever got here. She must just be used to things looking like hell because she sits in the mess all the time and it doesn't even bother her. All she's glad about is her brown flowered couch she can sleep on all day. Maybe it's her priorities that get all messed up. I know she cares about stuff. Like when she tells me to get my goddamn shoes off the coffee table or to put my goddamn shoes on when I go into the kitchen, which is something I can't figure on considering she's always barefoot and putting her feet wherever the hell it is she wants to put them. But that's Mom for you. Always a big contradiction when it comes to things.

I pass under the only thing there is that's hanging on the walls in the place which is a picture of the Virgin Mary holding a baby

Jesus. It's old and faded and has a couple of white creases running through it and there's not even a frame around it. It's hung right above the doorway that goes into the kitchen because of Mom saying she likes to be reminded of things. I don't know much on the subject because of Mom being tight-lipped about most things, but what I do know is that her mom gave it to her a long time ago. You know about as much as me on that one though. Not a whole heck of a lot really.

But just to suit my curiosity, I walk through the kitchen where the smell is even worse than it was when I walked through the front door. I look in the big pot on the stove. I have to breathe through my mouth because of if I breathe through my nose I might puke all over and make an even bigger mess. It looks like Mom tried to fry cabbage. It looks like she tried to fry it, but all she did was burn the crap out of it. It's still in there which I can't figure on considering if you mess something up, you throw it away. You get rid of it quick. Especially something that's smelling up the whole place. Who the hell fries cabbage for chrissakes. It smells like hell.

Anyways, right now I can't worry on how messy the place is, or what Mom tries to do and messes up. I could go on for days about that one. So I bend down and get a towel from under the kitchen sink where Mom keeps the rags and her million boxes of tissues and her rosary beads she got when she was little. I wet the towel in the sink so it's sloppy wet. What a place to put rosary beads. I don't have any rosary beads for my own, but I know that the last thing you do with rosary beads is put them someplace like under a disgusting sink. Who does something like that for chrissakes. Who does it and gets away with it. I'll tell you who. Mom that's who. She has excuses for everything, especially when it comes to a thing as crappy as putting rosary beads under a filthy sink even the bugs know to stay the hell away from. But that's Mom for you. And knowing her she'll get away with it like she gets away with everything else.

I need to get out of the kitchen before I pass out from the place smelling like hell. So I pass the back door that's always locked tight nowadays. I'd rather not ever walk by that damn door, but I have to considering it's the only way to get to my room. I go in the bedroom and shut the door quiet behind me. I don't need Mom on my case. The last thing I need is Mom to wake up and be angry because I woke her up from her time to sleep and get on my case. I'm just not up for it today. Her voice is nice, it's not that, but I don't like her riding me about stuff. She'd definitely ride me about the gun putting a cramp in her style. Mom's always in my way one way or another. Her and her crazy ideas. Who names their kid Dusty Sparrow for chrissakes. What's wrong with O'Malley anyways.

She's always in my way about something though. Like, I did have a friend for a while. A good friend. We were tight. That part I told you about before about nobody liking me because of my name, well, I stretched the truth some. Sometimes it happens. Anyways, he caught a thing for Mom and that ended it. I can't say I blame the guy for catching a thing for Mom. A lot of guys catch a thing when it comes to Mom. But the thought of him becoming one of those jokers from the shop, well, it was more than I could take. You can't keep being friends with somebody, even if you were tight, when you know how they've fallen for the wrong things in life.

His name was Dave. It still is, but I don't like to use it. Not that I have to considering he goes to the high school across town from mine. He still lives in that nice neighborhood I'm going to get into telling you about later. Sometimes things are easier when the guy you don't want to see goes to the high school way across town. But he was a cool guy, good and tough. Even his name sounded tough. Dave Treadway. If somebody tried to call him David or something he got angry and mean. Things like that set him off quick. His old man is the only one who gets away with stuff like that. His dad is a drunk. A scary drunk, so who could blame the guy for not standing up to his old man. They're rich so Mr. Treadway has money to buy the good stuff, and a lot of it. The kind of stuff that gets you good and smashed. I never even looked at the guy. He scared the hell out of me. But it was cool of Dave being friends with me like that considering I'm rough trade and he's not.

But it's disturbing to keep being friends with a guy who catches a thing for your mom, so you do what you have to do. To know what goes through a guy's head most times is enough to make you sick anyways, but to know those things somebody is thinking about your own mom, well, it was more than I could take. Dave's a smooth talker, too, and a good-looking sort of guy, so it gave me plenty of reason to worry. He talks good and proper like he should be the President of the stupid United States of America or something. He could talk the panties off any plain ordinary girl easy. And Mom is the way she is, so I just couldn't shake my bad feeling.

Who can like somebody that can't get your mom out of their head. Saying stuff like, let's eat over at your house again, even though I know when Mom cooks it tastes like hell and nobody can even stomach the food she makes. And then stuff like, your mom is a beauty a real beauty there Dusty boy. First of all, what kind of guy calls their friend Dusty boy, and second of all, what kind of a guy catches a thing for his friend's mom. It's wrong. It makes my ass bleed and my crap like vomit just thinking about it. I get a bad stomach when I think about Dave Treadway wanting to make Mom squirm like a little pig right under him. Just like all those jokers at the shop. Mom didn't really help things either by having a pretty face like she does. But I can't think on it now. To hell with Dave and Mom for that matter. You can't think on things that might get in the way of the good fortune you just happened upon.

CHAPTER SIX

I look back over my shoulder to make good and sure I shut the door to my bedroom tight behind me. I test it before I take the gun out of my pocket. Half of it is warm from being against my body. The other half is still cold from it being on the ground. It must've been there for a while for it to be so cold like it is. My blood is pumping good so I'm surprised I didn't heat the whole thing up. Who's to say how long it was there. Fall around here can be cold at times, and it's nice and cool today. I hold the warm part against my palm. I get all excited again. It's dirty and rusty, but it's a thing of beauty. No way in hell anybody's watching here so I can attend to my business. You can't see into my window from the street so even if the cars or the jokers or the college kids wanted to peek in they couldn't. My window faces that pile of wood that's next door, and nobody bothers with it because of it being just a pile of wood, so I know I'm good in here.

Those college kids can go to hell. Screw the jokers at the shop and the cars, too. What they don't know is good old Dusty Sparrow just won. What's wrong with O'Malley anyways. It sounds tough. But I guess having a stupid name doesn't matter much now anyhow considering I'm the one who's laughing. I may be laughing to myself right now and nobody but me knows it, but that won't last for long. Not with the prospects.

I start to get hot in my coat because of my excitement. I'm starting to sweat a little. I've had the same ugly blue and silver coat that I'm wearing since the seventh grade. I'm a sophomore now so it doesn't fit so good anymore and the silver isn't so silver. So I take off my coat and stand there in just my T-shirt holding the gun. It doesn't matter that it's in some bad shape right now. It's still a thing of beauty. It's the prospects that matter. I'll think of them in a minute. Just as soon as I'm not so hot.

I need to cool the hell off, so I sit down on the corner of my bed and breathe in through my nose and out through my mouth for a minute. But I can't stand just sitting there so I grab the wet towel. I start rubbing the barrel to get it clean. I start off slow at first, but keep getting faster the more I rub. There's a bunch of crap on my new good fortune, but it comes off pretty good if I rub long enough and fast enough. The towel I got from under the sink is still sloppy wet and drips right off my fingers and the gun and onto the floor. I don't care about the floor and the mess I'm making though, all I want is for the gun to be cleaned up nice. The floors in the place are a nice wood so I'm not worried about them making it. Floors like these here have been to hell and back, so a little water won't do a thing to hurt them.

I keep getting hotter with all the rubbing though. I've not cooled off one little bit. I know my face is red. My face always gets good and red when I'm hot like this. I think about taking a cold bath but decide against it. The place doesn't even have a shower so it would be a bath or nothing. I wouldn't know any better about having to take a bath if it wasn't for that nice place we stayed. That sure was a nice place. It had a shower where you could stand up with water that got hot and steamy and stayed hot the whole time you took your shower. Sometimes I'd shower three or four times a day just to stand under the hot water. But here, I don't hardly ever get clean here much less decide to sit in the tub to cool off in cold water. Who likes to take a bath and sit in their own filth in a tub that has rusty spots that have been there for who the hell knows how long. I don't. Besides, naked makes me sick. You have to be good and naked when you take a bath and look at your business just stare up into your face, so I avoid it most times. I'd like to cool off, but a bath is just not it.

It would be nice if I could open the window and get some fresh air, but it's painted shut with yellow paint so there's no opening it. It's nice and gray outside and I know like there's no tomorrow that the air is cool. It's only fall now like I told you before so old Jack Frost is just waiting to make his grand entrance like he does every year. Quiet, and then one day, bam. I can tell it's getting close to winter because of how gray it is outside. It's probably best I can't open the window anyhow considering the wood pile from that torn-down house next door that I was telling you about before is right outside my bedroom window. I guess I should be just as glad that my window doesn't face the shop, but I'm hot and want some fresh air. The air sure would feel good against my face right about now. But it's outside and I'm inside. So the only thing I can think of is to take my T-shirt off. I don't want to take it off, but I do it anyways. Naked makes me sick, so I try not to look at my chest if I can avoid it.

When I think on it I'm almost sure as I'm sitting here that the people who painted the room yellow must've done it because of it not getting much sunlight ever. Not even on the brightest days of the year can you tell when you're sitting smack-dab in the middle of my room that it's bright as hell outside. You know it's the daytime considering it gets lighter, but the sun just keeps its rays for the better half. There's close to 360 days of sunshine here in Colorado and I don't get to see a bit of it when I'm sitting in my room. There's hardly a day that goes by that the sun doesn't poke its head out of the sky. I guess it's pointless to think on it though considering it's just the way of things and they aren't going to change anytime soon as far as I can tell. I guess you do what you have to with paint. I'd rather not see the sun today anyways. The gray outside suits me just fine. I just wish like there's no tomorrow I could feel it on my face.

I try to forget about the dumb paint though and my bare chest, too, and try to think hard on all the good things that come along with finding a gun in your own yard. How many people do you know that appreciate a good thing when it comes along. I don't know many. I'd be willing to bet my cheap shirt I just took off that nobody would appreciate a good thing like I do like finding a gun in your yard. I'd bet my stupid shoes, and let me tell you something, there's nothing I don't like about my shoes so it's saying a whole bunch of things when I say it, but I'd bet my shoes that there isn't anybody that could tell the prospects like I can when it comes to this gun. Anybody else would've probably looked at the thing lying there in the leaves like it was, and just kick it out of the way like it was a measly rock that got in the way of where it was that they were going because of it being rusty and old. Most times people don't look twice at anything that's rusty. There might be a little more happiness around this stupid place if people did look twice at things and notice the prospects staring them right in their face.

Hell, just think on all the good things that would never come my way, which I know they will now like nobody's business, if I didn't keep my head about me and see all kinds of prospects right in front of me like if a big huge rock hit me smack-dab right between my eyes. I'm glad I didn't let the thought of the sonofabitch Mike poking his head out the front door of the shop again get in my head and ruin things. I can appreciate a good thing like nobody else appreciates a good thing. I'm going to clean this thing up so it's nice and cool. Let me tell you something, if you take the time to take something that's not nice to start with and make it nice, all kinds of good things will come your way. Like the prospects. Always think on the prospects.

So I rub for a long time. I don't even know how long. Sweat is dripping off my face and chest by now making a big mess on the floor. I'm hot and I can hardly stand it. I wipe my forehead with the back of my arm and it's sweaty. I look up for a minute and see my reflection in the window. It's gotten a little darker outside without my much noticing it and the nightlight that's in my room starts to shine from the corner. I can't see my face or anything like that, but I can see my outline plain as day. From the way it looks right now I can't tell where my hand ends and the gun begins just like it's been there my whole life. I look down at the gun again. It's cleaned up nice and fancy. I see a corner of my eye in the reflection. It shows off the blue cool. The gun's not perfect. I'm no fool. Hell, I'm not perfect either. But if I hold it just right and smooth nobody will know the difference. It's the prospects that matter. Not how dirty and rusty the thing is. And they're coming to me. The prospects are a thing of beauty, and they're coming to me.

CHAPTER SEVEN

It's been some time since that day when I came across my good fortune. I'm going to guess it's been several months, and everyday of those months have been the best days for me. Sure the same crap as always still goes on. But when you have the prospects you know you have them good and under your belt, so it's easier to get over the things that are good and rotten. Nothing has happened yet, but that doesn't mean I haven't felt good everyday that I carry the thing in my pocket. And there's not a day that goes by that it's not tucked in there good. I keep my hand right on it most times to remind me of things. Good things like the prospects. You always have to keep your eye on the prize.

So that's how we get to today. There's not too much important to get at about all those months between then and now, so I'm not going to get into it. If you want to hear about it you can ask me later, and I'll bore you to tears if you want. It was just the usual day in and day out kind of thing. Nothing all that interesting. That is until today. There's nothing usual about today. Today is what my whole life has been getting to. Right from the beginning this is where it's going. You don't happen upon a good fortune right in your own front yard if it wasn't supposed to happen just that way. So I'm on the right track as far as I can tell on things.

Today though I wake up earlier than usual. Not for any other reason than I just can't sleep anymore. As soon as my eyes pop open, I know like there's no tomorrow that today is like no other day. My stomach gets all tingly, like when you are just about to yak up a good one, and wakes me up. I'm still tired, but then again I'm always tired when I wake up. You can't get a good nights sleep living on the busiest street in town. There's hardly ever a time when something isn't going on, so you just have to work through it and grab some shut-eye even if you have to force yourself into it.

But I don't let something like getting only a little bit of sleep bug me today. Today I get up and get dressed quick just like I do every other day. I get dressed quick because I can't stand to walk even two steps from my bed without having my clothes on even if the only light in my room is coming from the nightlight in the corner. Sometimes I have no choice, but that doesn't mean I can't stand it. Naked makes me sick, but I can't sleep in my clothes because of then they won't air out. Nobody wants to wear clothes that haven't had the chance to air the hell out. I have to sleep mostly naked and I can't hardly stand it, but you do what you have to do. So I put on my usual to cover the hell up: jeans, T-shirt, my white and blue running shoes, and jacket zipped up all the way to the top with the gun in my pocket. I keep it simple. Always keep it simple.

The T-shirts I wear most times, well, they're from this place two places down from where we stay, one place across the street from the shop. It's a yellow house but nobody lives there, they just sell these T-shirts, so I don't know if it's a real house like you'd think. Sometimes you'd think they never leave the place considering they look wore out and wear the same things all the time, but I know they don't live there. It's not meant for anything but the T-shirts they sell. Anyways, I've been going there ever since I can remember to get the T-shirts for myself that these guys sell.

The place smells like hell because of the guys who own the place and sell the T-shirts are hippies, and hippies live for this crap called Patchouli. I know the name of it because of my asking them once what that crap was that made the place smell like hell. I didn't say it smelled like crap, I just asked what it was that the place smelled of. My curiosity just got the better of me on that one I guess. The Patchouli is supposed to cover up other stuff that smells like hell, but it only makes it worse. When I go in there it feels like I got a whole bunch of dirt stuck up my nose and can't get it out, and these hippie guys enjoy the hell out of it. They're nice enough so I don't mention that their Patchouli smells like hell. I just keep it to myself and try to make sure I don't breathe through my nose.

But I get my T-shirts there because of it being two doors down within easy walking distance. Besides that, the hippie guys caught a thing for Mom a long time ago so the T-shirts are free. You can just see it in their face when they ask something along the lines of, how's that mom of yours doing. I don't think about it much though considering it's best not to think about two guys thinking about your own mom. So when I go in to get my T-shirts I get to choose any one I want. There's not much choice though if you ask me. The T-shirts are all tie-dyed. There's not one that is just a plain old T-shirt. Who wants to wear a tie-dyed T-shirt anyways. They're ugly and don't look right on anybody, I don't care who you are. But when a T-shirt is free, you really can't be too choosy about it. You just learn to wear whatever the hell it is you have to put on.

The thing that gets me about it is how they hang three or four of their best T-shirts outside waving like some kind of hippie flag or something. They love the hell out of those things. Sometimes all you need to do is just understand what it is that somebody is into and let them be about their business. These guys are super into their T-shirts, so when I say I never want to tell them how I think they're ugly I'm telling the truth. Most times I try to find one that is faded. They look better on me when they're faded considering I look pretty faded myself with this ridiculous blonde hair and pale as hell blue eyes.

But today instead of putting on the tie-dye shirt like I usually do, I put on one of the white T-shirts I have from when we stayed in the nice place. The white ones are all about different things than the tie-dye ones. I even had to grab this one out of the top of my closet considering it's just not everyday you can wear the white T-shirt. Tie-dye didn't work with the nice place, and it's not going to work today.

You can't wear a tie-dye shirt when you want to look tough. You wear a white T-shirt with your jeans to look tough. And if the white T-shirt is a little dirty and stained like mine is, well, that's all the better. You know somebody is all about tough if they wear their T-shirt dirty. It's not that anybody ever sees what the hell my T-shirt is about anyhow considering I keep my jacket zipped to the top, but I know what it is a T-shirt is about, and I know what it is that's under my jacket. And sometimes you need to think on your own state of mind when it comes to things. So I put the white T-shirt on, zip my jacket up to the top like I said before, and get excited for the day.

The sun is barely up so I know Mom is still working her magic. Mom never makes it home much before eight o'clock. Sometimes those jokers at the shop occupy her until after I've gone to school. Those jokers, well, you don't see them all that often, but you know like the back of your hand that they're in there and what they're in there for. Anyways, you can't hardly see the sun from smack-dab in the middle of my room, but you can tell it's not so dark anymore. So it's half way between being super-dark and being light, so you know that it's early in the morning. At this time of day nothing is for sure. Things could go either way when it's this early. It's just a crap shoot.

I walk out of my room, through the house passing right through the kitchen because of my knowing there's nothing there anyhow, and straight through the front door that I don't close behind me. I do it out of habit even though I know Mom's not around to ride me about slamming the door and waking her up off the couch. Sometimes old habits die hard I guess. I cough a little when the air hits me because of it being cold outside. It's about as cold as it gets this time of year, but I don't mind it. The cold air gets good and in my lungs and makes everything inside seem to freeze right up, but I keep breathing it in deep because of the air smelling good and fresh like only morning air can.

The morning air always smells best on a Wednesday. You know it like the back of your hand when it's a Wednesday. There's just things your nose knows without really thinking too much on it. When you live someplace your whole life those things just kind of come all on their own. Your nose can tell you good the day before the slaughter smell comes from the town two or three towns away. It's kind of the darkest before dawn bit. Your nose can appreciate the smell of fresh air before it has to put up with the smell of burning blood. There's nothing like it. Like I told you about before, you never know if the air that smells like hell will hit you on Thursday or Friday, but you never take Wednesday for granted just to be on the safe side of things.

It's kind of a pisser to things when it gets cold out like it is now though considering my coat sleeves don't cover my wrists anymore because of my having had it since the seventh grade. There's no rips in it yet so Mom thinks it's good as new. She doesn't even think of the fact that it's too short in the sleeves to do much good. She doesn't even seem to care even though I've pointed it out good to her two or three times. It's a pisser when you have to shove your hands deep in your coat pockets just to keep your wrists warm. I do it fast because I'm cold. But I do it cool and smooth so nobody will get into their suspicions. People and their suspicions, there's really nothing like it. Always thinking that somebody like me is into something. The funny thing is that most times I'm clean when it comes to things. It's not me they have to worry about. It's people like that Brian Farrell that they need to worry about.

I look to my left at the shop and I know Mom is in there, and I know what it is that's keeping her in there if she's not already home by now. It makes me extra ill today just thinking on what it is that goes on right next door to my own house. I don't see any cars in the front, not that I really expect to anyways. You get a ugly reputation if you go in and people see you go in. There's a parking lot right in the front, but nobody parks there. Well, except for the old man. My father. Good old Dad. Whatever the hell you want to call him. It's your business. For a while there his car was parked right smack-dab in the middle of that stupid shop parking lot every stupid day of the week. No weekends, just during the week. Parked right in plain view of God and everybody. I still can't figure on which of the two is worse. You're going to have to make up your own mind on that one.

Word is, the old man is one of those smarties. You know one of those kinds that think for a living. You know the kind. He teaches at the college right across the street. Working with the college kids and trying to make our next goddamn President of the good old US of A. It must have been quick and easy, not to mention convenient, to just hop over to the shop considering it's right across the street from the college. Like right now if I wanted to I could chuck a rock across the street and it would land right on the lawn of the college. That's how close the stupid place is.

For being one of those smarties, he sure seems to be a dumb bastard. Even I have more sense when it comes to things than that guy. Everybody knew it was his car that he was parking there because of it being a plain-as-day noticeable red color with a white roof and white leather seats. On top of that, there were all kinds of smartie stickers plastered on the bumper that only those teachers have. Who would park their car right in the middle of the shop parking lot. All the other jokers know better. Even Mike the sonofabitch parks his car in the back in the alley I was telling you about, and he owns the place for chrissakes.

It's not a big place where we live, so how I know these things is because of word getting around quick. And the more juicy something is, the quicker it gets from here to there to there. I hear most stuff I don't know from other people and their kids who just happen to be my so-called peers. It's not stuff they tell you right to your face, it's the kind of stuff you hear floating around in the air like a leaf blowing in the wind or something. Sometimes even crappy people who like to get into their suspicions have their limits.

But it's easy to find out stuff if you want to. Like take my wanting to know about my so-called dad. You just have to open your ears when it comes to finding out things you're curious about.

People always talk, especially when it comes to rough trade. And Mom and me, we'll always be rough trade. Like I know the newspaper boy who delivers the newspaper every dumb day all around town doesn't come to our house on purpose. Something about his parents getting into their suspicions about how our block is a bad influence. That's not something somebody just walks right up and tells you to your face. You just hear things and then, bam, just like that, you know them like the back of your hand even though they might be a load of crap. But the thing around here is if somebody just says something, just mentions it like if you sneeze and you can't stop it, most people think it's gospel. It's just the way of things I guess.

It's a strange thing though these people around this place wanting to admit to a smartie from the college hanging out at the shop. Sometimes you'd think they'd rather cut off their right arm or something than admit to one of their smarties making a real mess of things. And good old Dad made a mess out of things for sure. Everything about around here is about the college. Most times people talk about the smarties like they own heaven for chrissakes. Nobody owns heaven though no matter what the hell anybody tells you.

But the thing about everybody knowing about my old man is a thing everybody knows, but a thing that's easily forgotten like if you got knocked over the head with a dirty two-by-four. I know and they know that it's the kind of information if left in the wrong hands, well, nasty things could happen in a town like Fort Harmony if the wrong person got a hold of it. Most times I wish I didn't know. Sometimes knowing things that are big like who the hell it is that's your father are things better left up to the imagination. At least with your imagination you can half-way stomach things considering you made them up in your head, and they may or may not be the way of things. But when you're rough trade, you don't get to choose the things you know, they choose you.

Anyways, screw the old man, and throw that paper boy in there while you're at it. I'm just glad right now that Mom's not here to get on my case. She's always riding me about something.

All I need this morning is some peace. All I need is for some time so that my lungs get used to the air that's cold going into them right now. I need it quiet. It's going to be a big day. I can feel it.

CHAPTER EIGHT

Things about today haven't exactly played out in my head, but like I said before, you can just tell when it's a big day. There's something in your blood that's different. I don't know how really. All I know is that it's different like if your insides got struck by static electricity that's running all the way through your whole body. And you know like there's no tomorrow when it's something big. Even when it's cold out like it is now, your blood is going fast. It's times like these here that you need to count your lucky stars for tipping you off to knowing the prospects and all the good things that are just waiting for you.

I'm standing on my front porch looking out at the day not knowing what to expect exactly and going over all the prospects one more time in my head. I've been thinking about them for months. I start rubbing the gun with my right hand. It's always in my right coat pocket considering you have to use the hand you write with to keep control if anything should pop up. I don't really know why I start doing it, but it's what I'm doing. My hands are already shoved in my coat pockets with it being cold, so it's not noticeable that I'm doing anything out of the day-to-day.

I'm glad Mom's not here because of I know she'd ride me about letting cold air into the house with my leaving the door wide open. If I close it and wake her up when she's on the couch she rides me, and if I leave it open like she always has it and let cold air into the house she rides me. You just can't win with her. It's always a lose—lose kind of a thing. She never shuts the dumb thing herself unless there's snow up to your hips outside, but with me, well, it's a whole different thing. She's always on my case. Just thinking on her makes my head flip. Why does it always come back to Mom. I wasn't even thinking on her and then, bam, just like that she's right the hell in my head. I turn around and close the door quick so I don't have to think on her anymore right now. It's best not to think on Mom whenever it is that you can avoid it.

I hear a train coming which breaks my concentration a little. By a little I mean it gets my mind off of things. There's trains that go in and out of this place at any time of the stupid day. I'm mostly used to it, but sometimes it just sneaks the hell up on you. There are some tracks close to where we stay so I hear them coming and going all the time. You can't see the tracks from our front porch, but you know like there's no tomorrow when it is that that train is coming. The tracks are only a little ways from the street where we live, and run right through the one side of the college, so when I say you can hear the trains good and loud you know I'm telling the truth.

Most times I like to hear the trains because of my knowing that they can go to places way the hell away from here. Trains can get good and far from places like Fort Harmony to places like Hollywood. It makes me think on again and again, every time I hear one, why Mom didn't hop one of those trains to Hollywood forever ago like she wanted to do in the first place. She was on her way. She just got caught here all because of a little stomachache from looking out the window for too long. And then I already told you about the rest after that. But that's Mom for you. Always missing what's right in front of her stupid face. Most times I like to hear the trains but sometimes, like late at night when I'm trying to get some shut-eye, the sound of the trains grates right against my bones. Right now though, I'm not thinking too much on the trains. It was a moment kind of a thing, and now it's over.

I guess I've been standing here for a while considering I start catching a glimpse out of the corner of my eye of all kinds of people walking across the street. I guess now is the time when people start moving for the start of the day. I've never paid much attention to it before. So I start watching them. I watch super-sly though. I'm looking at the college and what are obviously those college kids right smack-dab in the face. My stomach turns to hell right away. I have to pass that stupid place every stupid day of my life. I can't even step one stupid foot out of my house without having to see it. There's just no getting away from the smarties and their smart buildings and those smart clothes they all seem to know to wear.

I keep rubbing the gun in my pocket to keep from blowing my eyes right out of their sockets thinking on how much I can't stand them. I've been carrying this thing around in my coat pocket for months, and they don't even know it. Hell, they don't even know that I'm rubbing the thing right at this very minute. I know it makes me look tough and smooth. I've been practicing how to stand just right like I am now everyday since I found the thing. Things like this take practice. I've watched myself in windows and mirrors, so I know that what I'm saying is the truth. The cool part about it is, nobody but me knows it's there. Nobody but me knows I'm in control. I dare someone to caw at me now. I dare those college kids to pretend I'm not here.

It's mighty studious of them getting up early in the morning like this just to go learn things they don't need to know. My stomach turns to hell just looking at them, but I stare at them and I don't look down. If things were different than they are then maybe I would be walking on the other side of the street with those college kids instead of standing where I am. Hell, I have a smartie for a dad. I'm no fool you know. I know all sorts of things about this world the smarties would pay to know. But who wants to be a college kid anyways. I can't stand those pompous college kids. See I told you I know things. Not everybody can just come up with a word like pompous like they just sneezed all over their shirt or something.

I can't believe the things that are going on right now. They're still ignoring me for chrissakes, and I'm just right across the street. I get tense. I'm staring them down good. Nothing. My anger starts getting the better of me. I rub the gun harder. I rub and rub and rub till my finger tips feel smooth then I walk the hell across the street. I don't think about doing it. I just do it like somebody wound me up and let me go.

I juke the cars that come fast. They're coming quick like they are trying to hit me or something. But I don't let them. I'm a pedestrian for chrissakes. It's not like they don't see me. How could they not see me with all this blonde hair practically blinding them. There's just general rules everybody has to follow and not hitting pedestrians is one of them. But I don't lose my temper. I keep my head cool and my walk smooth. Let me tell you something, it's not easy to do when you're dodging cars all because of you not having any other choice in the matter. I do good considering my anger and how it's just boiling out of control under my skin.

My face is hot. I know it's red. The air feels good and cool against my face. I'm on the other side of the street by now and out of traffic. I just need to calm myself down and catch my breath. I could take my coat off, but I keep it zipped to the top. I need to think about the prospects, and the minute you unzip your coat and take it off, well, you'd better just throw in the towel. Always think of the prospects. Today people will know Dusty Sparrow won. So, instead of just standing here trying to catch my breath like a little girl or something, I start walking again like I know what the hell it is that I'm doing. You need to do that sometimes to make sure everything looks on the up-and-up. You can't ruin things all because of you just standing there drawing attention to yourself.

It's a beautiful thing walking on the curb with these college kids. I'm walking right next to them and they still ignore me. I almost laugh out loud because it's so obvious, but I don't considering I don't want to startle the situation. You don't want to shake things up before you are good and ready for them. Like take this girl here. I'm walking right next to this one girl with her hands in her pockets, too. She has super-short hair. It's pitch black and boy-like and has no shine to it. Her ears are red considering how cold it is right at this particular moment. She's short and I can see the top of her head because of my being pretty tall. I've always been taller than my peers and they still irritate me. Who would figure on that one. You'd think it's only the small guys that get irritated, but that's not the case here.

But with the girl with the black hair, well, I watch her for a long time all noticeable. I stare her down good, and she still ignores me. I'm looking right down at the top of her head with all my might. Can't you tell when somebody is staring you down good. I can. My back gets stiff. It's hard and straight because of the college kids ignoring me. Like they are the only ones in the world worth a damn. Not a one of them has bothered to even look at me. It just about makes your ass hair curl from things being the way they are with the college kids around here.

Right now I could blow off a little steam with this girl and her short black ugly hair. But the problem when it comes to me is I get mad but I don't say anything to anybody. All I can figure on is that when you're rough trade like I happen to be, you could walk down the street pretending like you're the President of the US of A or the Pope and nobody will even look at you sideways much less listen to a stupid thing that comes out of your mouth. When you're rough trade, everybody knows it and you need to know it, too. There doesn't seem to be a whole lot of breaks out there for us. When I get mad at things I could talk until I'm blue in the face, or yell until my stupid head shoots straight off my neck, and still nothing. Not a damn thing. Not even a flinch from anybody. Nothing. These senseless people I'm stuck with. I just can't stand it sometimes.

But the good thing about me is that I realize now's the time to make it a whole different ballgame. I'm cocked and ready to go. Things are turning around quick. Like I said before, things just don't walk up and give you everything you've ever needed for the prospects, like what happened with me and the gun, so you need to get the ball rolling when you see the opportunity. I should take advantage of my good luck. Maybe now with the prospects like they are I can get mad about things that are wrong with the world and somebody is going to have to perk up their stupid ears and learn the hell how to listen. Beautiful.

The first person today that's going to get an earful is going to be this girl with the black ugly hair that's walking right next to me. She's walking on my right side so it's convenient for things when they go down. I have a whole mouthful to say to her. She's making my blood super-hot all because of she's still ignoring me, and I'm still staring her down good. I have to look away to get what I want to say squared away in my head. I'm not so good with these kinds of things, so I have to think extra hard to calm myself down and come up with what the hell it is I want to say. So I'm going to say, what makes you think you're better than me, and pull my gun out and watch her eyes get big when they have to look right the hell at me. I can see it all happening plain as day in my head.

I turn to say it all, I have it down good, but she's gone. I know she was right next to me though. She was right there. I guess it's probably best that things worked out like this considering I'm nervous, and every stupid word would've probably been one long stutter. Nobody wants to stutter when they're saying something important. I tell myself that the day has just begun, and it's better to save things for the right time. You need to know when to cut your losses, and right now's a good time to start practicing. There's more time than you'd think for things to work out the way you'd hope they'd turn out.

Funny thing is I keep walking with the other college kids going to class, and before I know it I find myself right in the middle of the campus. It doesn't take long to get here considering my house is right across the street, but this wasn't where I meant to go. I don't know exactly where it is I was going, but I don't think it was here in the middle of the stupid college campus. I guess I just got caught in the crowd without much thinking on it.

I'm hot because of my anger with that girl, but I don't let it bug me. It's the prospects that count. For some reason I keep going along the campus like my feet take over or something. I start walking fast but smooth. I put it in my head a long time ago what class my old man teaches. A useless smartie that guy. I figure what the hell. I'm already this far anyhow. So it doesn't surprise me when I wind up sitting smack-dab in the middle of a classroom with good old Dad standing up in the front. He looks studious. Like a goddamn stand-up kind of a guy.

I know the classroom and its whereabouts all because of I heard that sonofabitch Mike riding Mom once about pumping the smartie for money. He said that that's what you do with somebody who knocks you up. Mike the sonofabitch knew he'd do anything to avoid a sticky situation so why not. Those smarties would do anything to keep hold of their so-called reputation, they'd hold on right by their teeth if they have to. Mom tried to change the topic fast because of it being one of those times I was behind the counter. But he kept spilling it like he was some kind of radio guy or something talking about the weather. So it's been good and in my head since then. He was on Mom's case that day. Thinking back on it, I'm surprised as hell Mom didn't take Mike the sonofabitch up on what he was saying. It would stop all the lottery tickets and the hoping that she does.

Anyways, back to the story. Always keep to the story. I take a seat in the middle of the classroom with the college kids, and they're still ignoring me. They're all looking straight the hell forward, and not even noticing that I came around. I decide just to say to hell with them and look right in the old man's face. I keep it cool. I see him see me, and he ignores me, too. He looks right at me for chrissakes. The tingles in my stomach start up again. The gun is warm in my right hand. I grab it smooth in my palm. They're not going to ignore me anymore, not today, that's for sure. I'm making damn sure of that.

He starts talking all of his smart talk right away, even before everybody can grab a seat. Looking at the guy I can just picture the things that happened in the shop, and how I came into things. A smartie like him would find all kinds of beauty in a face like Mom's. It sure is different from the books he usually has his nose buried in. It's not hard to imagine how he got overworked and wrecked by one of the magazines, and did what we all know he did to Mom right there on that counter. That's the way I hear it goes anyways. That's what Mike the sonofabitch and people around town say, and it's hard not to believe the things you hear when you half want to believe them.

You just want to know about your dad when you don't know anything about him for your whole life and Mom, well, Mom doesn't tell me stuff because of it being her business. Mom rides me when I try to talk about it though, and I do try to talk about it considering it's how I came into things. A simple yes or no would do the trick. Is that so hard to come up with. A stupid yes or no. But Mom, well, she'd just rather play like she and the Virgin Mary have a lot in common. But they don't have a lot in common. Not a simple thing really and just to prove it I'm sitting here looking right into the face of the man who makes it so. She's no Virgin Mary, and I'm no baby Jesus.

I know the way the story goes is probably the truth considering I've seen plenty of no good on that counter before. Mom's pretty. Pretty but loose. Slutty if you want to get down to it. I wouldn't put much past her. Word is that the smartie never went back after that time considering he had a reputation to think of. It would definitely ruin things if it was found out by the wrong kind of people what he did with rough trade in the shop. The college kids would like that story, but they don't know about those kinds of things because of them being the wrong kind of people. So I plan on saying all of it, about what he did with the floozy from the shop, and about what came out of it. The look on their faces when they hear what the bastard is really all about is going to be a thing of beauty.

I stand up slow and quiet, and I keep my hands in my coat pockets. I stare at the old man and don't look down. He sure is a short bastard. And ugly, too. There's something odd looking about him that I can't quite put my finger on just yet. His hair isn't even a color really. It's super-dull. He's old, too, and wears a lot of corduroy like all the other smarties around this place. I hate corduroy. And the glasses. I'm not even going to mention the glasses. He looks at me and says a few big words. Always being studious because of that being the way it is with smarties. He's polite enough when he asks if I have a question, but I get sick and disgusted all of a sudden. What kind of guy is he. Pretending he doesn't know me. I look just like her for chrissakes, and I doubt he forgot about her. You just don't forget about Mom. If you ever knew her, she's in your head for good. I look just like her.

The college kids look up. Right on cue like everything the guy says is gospel. All of them look up. I keep staring, and I feel my face get hot again. I know it's red. A smile comes to the old man's face. It's a polite enough smile, but I can't stand it anymore with my being hot and that fake as hell look on his face. I'm going to let him know the way of things. I take my right hand out of my coat pocket holding the gun smooth. Only, as the crapper of things that are happening here, my hand is wet from being sweaty. The stupid thing slips as soon as I pull it out and makes a loud noise when it hits the floor and slides under one of the college kid's desks. It makes a loud noise in a room that's completely quiet by now and startles me like nothing else ever has. I was ready, prepared to hold the thing steady right into that smile I now see is fake on the old man's face. You know, to kind of say, fuck you for not owning up to responsibilities. I had it all planned on what I was going to say to ruin things good for good old Dad, and let the college kids know just what the hell he's made of. That is until the stupid thing slips out of my hand and slides across the stupid floor.

So I know nobody can ignore me now. It's the timing of things that seems to be the real crap shoot though considering now I wish they would ignore me so when I bend down to crawl across the floor and get my gun, like I know I'm going to have to, I could do it in some privacy. If they stared and I was holding the thing smooth it would be a thing of beauty, but right now is a whole other thing. I can just picture how all these stupid college kids would panic and dive to the floor and run out of the room like a scared squirrel will run across the street to keep from being hit by a car. And I know all about those stupid cars. Not that I could do anything anyways with the gun being dead, but it would've been a thing of beauty to sit back and watch the panic.

My face is hot, maybe even a little worse than before, and I start to feel sweat running down my back. But I don't concentrate on it now because I have to get my gun. Everybody is still staring, but I don't have any other choice than to get on my knees and grab the thing. I can't just leave all my prospects laying there under a desk like that. You never leave your prospects. A couple of the girls way behind me get freaked out and start crying loud. Leave it up to worthless girls to freak out like that. I didn't do a damn thing really. But I need to get out of the room fast because of them crying and it getting good and under my skin. So I get the gun and tuck it under my arm, get the hell up off my knees, and run out of the room fast. The old man just stands there dumb like he's holding his pecker in his hand. What a disgusting pansy.

CHAPTER NINE

I'm out of the building by now, and I can hardly breathe. I high-tailed it pretty quick to get out of there fast. You can't dilly-fart around when stupid girls start in on their crying. It'll get you nowhere fast considering everybody will do anything to get a crying girl to shut the hell up. It's a shame I couldn't say what I wanted to say to that bastard. Things just weren't meant to work out that way I guess. But for some reason, even though things seem good and ruined right now, I get all excited all of a sudden. A real thrill if you want to know the truth. They noticed me. They all had to perk the hell up and pay attention to things I'm all about. They noticed me. I know like there's no tomorrow nobody can ignore good old Dusty Sparrow anymore.

But even with that being the case, I start off the campus fast. I plan to lay low for the rest of the day because of my knowing what I did back there is a serious thing to do. I know I'm not going to get caught considering I did what I did on the good side of the street where things don't usually happen, but I run anyways. I run cool though so I don't attract attention that I don't need. It sure is lucky for me having my running shoes on. Like I told you about before, the shoes and the gun are a match made in heaven. I knew they would be handy some day, and that day seems to be today.

I'm running cool, and I'm thinking about all of their faces. What a thing to know that nobody but me knowing not one little thing was going to happen to them and their lives. I know it was only a second, seeing that look I'm talking about, but you only need a second to have a thing of beauty burned right in your brain for good. I wish that girl with the ugly short black hair would come around now. I sure as hell wouldn't lose her a second time around. But I can't think on that. I'm going to lay low. I'm just taking extra precautions right now to keep the prospects good and safe. The college kids and the smarties don't worry about crap happening. They're never prepared for crap. The stupid girls crying. Leave it to the girls.

By now I'm far enough away from where it is I'm trying to get away from, so I stop running. Things are pretty much deserted now outside, so I'm not worrying a whole lot anymore. It's starting to warm up outside. Not much but a little. It's getting hard to see my breath. Pretty soon it's going to be gone altogether. Spring around here is a funny thing. It's cold in the mornings and then just like that it starts getting warm. I'm getting hot now in my coat and don't need to keep out the cold anymore, but I keep it zipped to the top. I keep my hands deep in my pockets.

I start across the street like I'm going home without much thinking on what I'm doing, but I turn quick right the hell around because of I see the front door to where we stay open wide. I know that I closed that thing behind me so it can only mean one thing, and that thing is that Mom must be home. The last thing I need is for Mom to get on my case about not being at school. She'd ride me about needing it quiet so she can sleep. Like school does me any good. Who needs a useless education anyways. I need to lay low, that's what I need right now, to lay low and sly. I need to keep quiet for the rest of the day. It's times like these I wish Dave Treadway and I were still cool. We were cool for a while, super-tight the two of us. It's times like these I wish he was still around. He'd appreciate the hell out of the beauty of what just happened.

So I don't go home and I'm not going to school. I need to lay low. I stay walking on the one side of the street keeping my head down with my hands deep in my pockets. The gun is getting warm again and I keep rubbing it with my right hand. It feels good. My stomach gets tingly like it did when I woke up. I can hardly stand my excitement. I walk far and I'm super-hot. I decide to walk through Old Town past all the shops. I can't go in a one of them to cool off because they're all closed considering it's still early in the morning as far as the shops are concerned. I start to sweat a little more, but I keep my walk cool and smooth because of my not wanting to draw attention from anybody.

I'm walking a little too fast though by my estimations. It's like I'm trying hard to get away from what the hell I don't know what of. I guess right now it just feels like the natural thing to be doing. I'm walking along minding my own business when I catch sight of myself in the long hardware store window. I can't help but stop. The only thing I want to do is pick my feet the hell up and get out of here, but for reasons I don't know I stop right in front of the window. I look tall and tough standing here. Nothing like that short bastard. I look tough with my chin tucked in the top of my coat. I keep it zipped to the top even though the sun gets hotter with each passing second. My hands are still deep in my pockets. I keep my right hand on the gun. You can't even see it in my pocket. Nobody but me knows I've won. I'll tell you one thing for sure, it's going to be hard laying low because of there still being prospects out there just waiting for their moment. And that moment seems to be right around the corner so far as I can tell.

The trouble with right now is all the cars driving by. I was telling you about the cars before. They break into my concentration like it's their business or something. It's not their business though. My business is my business, and right now I just need some peace and quiet. It's a momentous occasion, and I can't even enjoy it properly. There are a lot of cars because of it being the time when everybody has to get somewhere important, and because of my being on the busiest street in town. I see every single one of them in the hardware store window as they drive right behind me. They're nice ones, too. The cars is what I'm talking about. It makes me think I could use one of those nice cars right about now. It would open up a whole new world considering the prospects. A getaway car would be a thing of beauty.

I could steal that sonofabitch Mike's car from the alley if I wanted to, but it's a piece of crap. You can't have a piece of crap getaway car because of there being no guarantees that it would run. I could steal it easy though without much of an effort. He doesn't even lock the thing. It would be easy, but there's one thing I know for sure about these kinds of things, you can't have a piece of crap getaway car. Things might get ugly. In fact, things are bound to get ugly.

I'm not old enough to drive anyways. It's not like I could get into a car, even one of the nice ones, and know whatever the hell it is you're supposed to know on how to drive the thing. Most of my so-called peers will be able to drive by the end of the year, and I know like there's no tomorrow most of them will be getting nice cars right at their fingertips. I know that stupid Brian Farrell will be getting a gem of a car. It's funny how you can be rotten like he is and get a nice car just because you breathe in and out everyday and your dad just happens to own a successful business of something that nobody knows for certain. I'm sure it'll be a dainty car, nothing like I'd ever pick out to drive that's for sure. Dave Treadway already has his license because of him being older than myself. He drives a hell of a nice car. He told me I could drive it once, but I said no considering you don't want to mess up another guy's car especially when you don't have your driver's license.

But that driver's license will never come my way. There's just things you can count on and that's one thing I can count on, my not getting my driver's license. There's two good reasons why. The first being that I really don't see worth a damn. Nobody would ever give anybody a driver's license who can't even see who the hell it is that's looking at them half the time much less little tiny letters you're supposed to make out on a wall way the hell across the room. What kind of mom won't get her kid glasses for chrissakes. What an idea, thinking only crazies wear glasses. I guess I'll never know where she gets her ideas from.

Anyways, the second thing is that there's no car in my life. How the hell are you supposed to drive when there's no car in your life. The sonofabitch Mike told me once that I could use his car if I wanted to, you know in one of his getting a thrill out of pretending he's my dad moments. But I told him I wouldn't piss in the same pot as him much less drive around in his crappy car. The things that guy says sometimes. You know they're just to get things for himself and nobody else. It sounds like he's on the up-and-up, but you have to know better. I guess acting the way he acts is normal for a sonofabitch like Mike though.

Screw the cars. I have enough to think on right now than to keep concentrating on fancy cars I'll never drive. So I walk on. What else are you supposed to do in these kinds of situations like I have here. You can wish as hard as you want on things being different than they are, but that doesn't mean a goddamn thing when it comes to things. I've wished hard on things all my life, and I don't have a thing to show for it. Not one thing. Like, take the little tiny baby that was supposed to come into things a long time ago. I prayed to God everyday for that little tiny baby because of Mom telling me it was the right thing to do for somebody about to come into the world. She even taught me how to make the sign of the cross good so God couldn't miss it. I was good at it, too, making the sign of the cross, and I'm sure I said all the right things in those prayers I made, but it turns out praying is just like wishing. Nothing good seems to come of it. Just look at the facts now and you'll know like there's no tomorrow that what I'm telling you is the truth. There's no little tiny baby that came into things even if I did make the sign of the cross good so God couldn't miss it. Period. End of story. I don't like that that's the way of things, but that's just the way they are.

So I just keep walking on considering I can make myself mad quick if I don't watch it. I rub the gun in my pocket with my thumb. All my other fingers are too sweaty to budge even one tiny bit considering I learned my lesson back at the stupid college on how sweat can mess up things good and quick. My thumb though, well, I can use my thumb to rub along the thing and know there's still a thing of beauty about today. Good old Dusty Sparrow has finally won. Like I said before, it's not worth much, but it still sure is nice.

By now I'm standing right smack-dab in front of this jewelry shop. I can know it's a jewelry shop because of all the small cushy black display things that could only hold something small like a pretty ring or something. There's no ring in there now considering the shop isn't even open yet, but there's just things you know and right now that's what I know. But my attention gets broken because, just like somebody crapped themselves or something, somebody starts laying on the horn. Just like that and, bam, I can't get away from the jewelry shop fast enough. I would hate for anybody to get into their suspicions with me standing in front of the jewelry shop looking in like I am especially with somebody laying on that goddamn horn like they are.

I start running back towards the college and try to go fast, but it's hard to go fast with one hand in your coat pocket. They won't get off that loud as hell horn. Don't they know they could mess up the prospects if they keep laying on the horn like that drawing attention to a situation that doesn't need attention. Especially not at this particular damn moment. The last thing I need is the stupid police poking around wondering about things like my hand in my coat pocket all because of somebody not knowing when to lay off their horn.

Then I think better of things and stop running and turn back the hell around. You draw more attention to yourself when you run, and like I told you about before, the last thing I need right now is attention from anybody. Especially not those smarties back at the college who might've figured some things out by now. So I re-cross the street I just ran across two seconds ago, and I do it calm and cool.

Besides the obvious things happening at the moment to crap things up, my feet hurt like hell. The running shoes that are meant for running, well, let me just say they don't do a thing as far as running goes. That stupid somebody is still laying on the horn like there's no tomorrow, but I've gotten farther away so it doesn't break into my head so much as it did when I was closer. Funny how some people try hard to draw attention to a situation that probably doesn't have anything to do with anything. Some people. Who knows where the hell it is they learn to think anyways.

CHAPTER TEN

I keep walking cool so I don't draw any more attention from the cars. It's not so easy to do when your ticker is going like a bat out of hell still from all the commotion that that one person caused with their stupid horn. I breathe in deep to try and calm my heart down a bit. I do it without being obvious about it. But it's a funny thing about around here how you can draw attention to yourself when you've stopped running and you're just walking there not doing a thing but walking there. So I need to pay extra attention to what it is I'm doing. I need to melt right in with the sidewalk is what I need to do.

One good thing is that there's nobody else walking the street with me. They're all in cars getting to where it is they need to go. I'm glad because of then I don't have to look anybody in the face. Not that I ever really look anybody in the face considering most times it's just easier not to. But today, right now especially, I'm thinking it might be obvious that I'm trying not to look so I'm glad it's just me on the sidewalk. I'm just glad I don't have to worry about anybody else right now. The cars are enough to drive you out of your head all on their own.

Most of the shops are still closed, but I see one on the same side as where I'm walking that has one of its doors wide open. It's a gypsy looking shop just a little ways up from this ice cream shop that has good and tasty ice cream. I've never been inside the gypsy shop, and I only had the ice cream in the ice cream shop once. It was when Mike the sonofabitch took me there to try hard on being my dad or something. Mom never told Mike the sonofabitch to do it, it was all his own idea. He just came into where we stay and said, put your goddamn shoes on. He said it just like that, too. He said it was time to teach me a thing or two about being a man.

Some people think Mike the sonofabitch is crazy. People do that sometimes to give other people some kind of excuse for being a super-crappy sonofabitch. Regular people especially do that. You know, they like to think people like Mike the sonofabitch are crazy or else why would they act like they act. It helps them not get mad at crappy people, you know with the whole idea of humanity weighing on them like a ton of bricks. It makes you wore out when you get mad at people so I can't say I blame them much.

But as far as I go, I know like there's no tomorrow Mike's a sonofabitch because of him liking the way he is. You have to watch a guy's mouth to know if they're a real live crazy or not. And him, well, I don't trust his mouth. He has a good time with things that are enough to make you sick. You know, laughing hard at things with his mouth open wide so you can see his big fat tongue rub up against his crooked teeth. I hate big fat tongues, and crooked teeth, too, for that matter. His teeth are about as crooked as he is. You should've seen the way he went to town on that ice cream. If it wasn't so tasty I might not ever want to eat it again after what I saw going on in his mouth.

It makes it hard to sleep at night when you know there are crappy people out there who want to be crappy. It makes it ten times as hard when you have to know the guy and see how it is that he snows these people. Most times I wish I could do what regular people do and make up excuses for that sonofabitch Mike. But it's hard to do when you know the things I know. As far as Mom goes though, everything that sonofabitch says is like gospel. She might as well get down on her knees and pray to the guy the way she does when she wants something from God. It's basically what she does anyhow, so I think she should just go all the way with it.

What a thing for him to think he'd know the first thing on how to be a man. But you don't not go with somebody when they own the place where you stay, even if it is somebody like Mike the sonofabitch and you'd rather do anything than go. So I did what he told me to do and I put my goddamn shoes on even though I wanted to tell him to go to hell like nobody's business. Most times I can do it without thinking twice on the whole thing, but when I think back on it I must've been good and curious not to do it when I wanted to bad. I guess I just wanted to know what kind of crap Mike the sonofabitch could come up with about knowing about being a man.

He's just your average, everyday, run-of-the-mill sonofabitch that doesn't even know how to clean himself much less know the way of things. Some days I'd bet my shirt that guy'd rather roll around in cat piss than take a shower for chrissakes. Like I told you about before, he's always wearing the same pair of pants and they smell like hell. He sure is a sonofabitch. He couldn't be anybody's dad in a million years. Not even with mint chocolate chip ice cream. But I sure did like the ice cream anyways even if I did have to shut the hell up and just let Mike the sonofabitch run his mouth the way he likes to. The things you'll do for a tasty ice cream.

But I can't think on ice cream now. It might help if the ice cream shop was open to cool me down though. I'm hot and I can hardly stand it, and someplace that's cool where I could get some of this heat out of me sounds pretty good right about now. I still remember how good it felt to walk in the place after the ride that seemed like forever in Mike the sonofabitch's crappy car. It was a hot sunny day, and Mike the sonofabitch has a thing about rolling down the windows. And besides not being able to roll the windows down, I'll bet anything that a crappy car gets hotter than a nice car any day of the week. It's just the way of things. I want to go into the ice cream shop more than ever considering I'm about ten times as hot as that now. But it's not open, so I just need to put it out of my mind.

So I look in the window to the gypsy shop. I look in for one good reason and that's because of it being open. I see a lady in there fixing up the gypsy things. I open the glass door, the one side of the door that's not already open, slow but confident. You get what you want with confidence. Besides, I don't want to scare the hell out of the lady by just popping up on her from out of nowhere. A little bell rings, and the lady looks up from what she's doing and says hello right away. Just like that she says hello. That's all I ask is for people like those stupid college kids to say hello like this nice lady and not ignore me like they like to do. They're not the only ones in the world worth a damn. Not today anyways. Good old Dusty Sparrow is worth a damn today.

She looks at me kind of funny like she can't tell if I heard her nice hello, so I say hello back in a nice voice. I didn't mean to stand there for too long, but I was just appreciating the moment. She asks if there is anything I need help with and her voice is still nice like it was when she first said hello. I keep it cool when I ask if I can use the bathroom. She says, sure help yourself, and points to the back of the store down this skinny hall. I say, thank you, remembering my manners and ask in a polite way if she has some scissors I can borrow. She looks at me funny but smiles anyways, and then goes behind the counter to get me the scissors I asked for. Her teeth are yellow, but she has a nice smile besides her teeth being yellow. She hands me the scissors, and I grab them with my left hand. I have to because of my right hand being busy holding the gun in my coat pocket. I say, thank you again, and walk to where she pointed for the bathroom.

Mom would hate that I stopped in a place like this one here. It would get under her skin good and quick if she knew I stopped in a place where there's nothing but gypsy kinds of things all over the place. The Virgin Mary is nowhere to be found. Mom would have a field day with that one considering she thinks a place without the Virgin Mary or Jesus on the cross is a no good place. There's plenty of places that don't have the Virgin Mary or Jesus on the cross anywhere in sight and Mom doesn't say a thing. Like I know that there's no Virgin Mary or Jesus on the cross in the gas station just up from where we stay, and Mom is in there all the dumb time buying those stupid lottery tickets with her slutty money. She doesn't seem to have any problems with that one. But I know like there's no tomorrow this is the kind of place she'd find a whole mouthful wrong with. I don't have problems with it though. The walls in here are a dark purple. It's the same color the sky gets on a good day just before it gets black and all the stars come out, so how could you not think a place is OK with walls like that.

I know Mom would have problems because of my knowing her well. Who the hell knows where she gets her ideas from anyways. I'm not even going to mention how she would ride me about not being in school. She can't hardly stand it when she can't keep good tabs on my whereabouts. Not that she keeps good tabs on me anyways, but I don't want to be the one to break that to her. Things might get good and ugly if she knew the tabs she thinks she's keeping on me are way off the mark. If I think on it I can know that she is happy when I just keep the hell out of her hair. But anyways, I said I'm not going to mention it so I'm not. There's more important things in the works right at the moment so I'm going to concentrate like nobody's business on those things. Life is a thing of beauty sometimes. Sometimes you just have to clear your head to see things clean.

Beautiful.

I get to where I'm going which is the bathroom. It looks clean in here but I can tell that that's just the way things look. The floor is black with white flecks all over it so it doesn't show much of what's going on with the dirt and things that I don't want to know about. It smells like the floor of the shop in here. I know the smell of that place good considering how much time I spent crouched on that floor. I'd sit behind the counter where the cash register is. I sat on my heels and hugged my knees whenever it was that I was behind that counter.

I'd sit there and hear the men come in, and Mom would talk to them nice and sweet. It was always men. Never women. She has a nice voice. It can be soft when she wants it to be. I couldn't see her, but I just knew she was smiling big at the jokers like she smiles big at Mike the sonofabitch. I'd sit there on the floor and not even sneeze if I had to because of it would be bad for business if they knew a kid was there. That's what Mom said anyways. I knew those jokers could really give a damn if there was a kid there or not no matter what Mom said. It's enough to make you sick sometimes. But those jokers, nothing makes them sick.

When you're a kid and your mom works at the shop, where else are you supposed to go. Your mom is your mom, right. When you're a kid and your mom tells you to sit behind the counter and be quiet, you do it. Nobody, I don't care who you are, wants their mom on their case about not sitting behind the counter and being quiet like she said. Besides that, when your mom tells you something, you buy it just because she's your mom and you trust her.

Anyways, that's the last time I want to talk anything about that considering it gets good and in my head when I think on it even for a second and it's hard to shake it once it's there. It's hard with me being in this bathroom smelling like it does, but I have more important things to think on right now. Let me tell you something, nobody, I don't care who you are, wants to see their mom do the kinds of things I saw Mom do when I was behind that counter. It's all kinds of ugly that won't get out from under your skin. It's enough to turn your stomach to hell for a good long time. So that's it. Over and out.

I feel my shoes start to stick to the smell right now that's on the floor of the gypsy lady's bathroom. Now I know for sure that the floor is good and disgusting. It's annoying having your shoes stick to the floor, but the last thing you want to do in these situations is take your shoes off. There's no telling what the hell will eat through the soles of your feet, so it's best to keep your shoes laced right to the top even if they do stick to the floor. The last thing you want is something eating at the bottoms of your feet for chrissakes.

Anyways, I clear my head and look in the mirror. It's dirty like the kind of dirty that takes years of ignoring it to get that way. I can't stand it so dirty, so I wet my hand in the sink and wipe it over the mirror. I use my left hand again for the reasons I told you about before. All I do is smudge the dirt around in circles, but I like the way my face looks. It looks old and tough. I look at myself for a long time. I'm still hot. In fact I keep getting hotter by the second.

When I get hot like I am now one of the things I can do to cool the hell off is to cut my hair. Like I told you before, my hair is ridiculous blonde. Albino-like and straight, too, just like Mom's. Most times it doesn't irritate me because of my not paying too much attention, but if it gets too long and too goddamn hot I cut it off myself. It looks like hell when I do it. Mom gets good and on my case when I do it. She cuts it herself most times and does an OK job. But when I get hot, there's not really any other choice in the matter. That's why I wanted the scissors and the lady was nice enough not to even ask. She just handed them to me like I had nothing on my mind.

When we were living in the nice place, in the good part of town like I told you about before, Mrs. Treadway would cut my hair. She'd give me a nice haircut, too. Dave would always leave us alone when she mentioned I needed a haircut because of him thinking it was boring watching a guy get his haircut. It sure was a thing of beauty when she'd give me haircuts. She's a stand-up lady. She even told me to call her by her first name because of my calling her Mrs. Treadway made her feel old. She said it just like that, old, so she said to call her Peggy. But I had a hard time with that considering how much of a stand-up lady I think she is. So to keep everything smooth and respectful, I just started saying Mrs. Peggy Treadway.

Anyways, she cut my hair a few times when we lived in the nice place and what I remember most is Mrs. Peggy Treadway's pearls. She's always about pearls. I've never seen her without them around her neck. You know somebody has to be like a gem on the inside if they know how to wear pearls and have them look like they're meant to be there. She even wore a pearl ring that she probably bought right out of one of those display things at the jewelry shop I was telling you about. Most people

I come into contact with don't even know what the hell the stink is about jewelry much less be able to appreciate a classy thing like pearls.

Mrs. Peggy Treadway always smelled good, too, and her own hair looked nice and classy. I thought she cut it herself considering she knew how to give a good haircut until one day I asked her if she cut it herself and she said no. Most times I feel dumb if I figure somebody wrong like I figured Mrs. Peggy Treadway wrong, but with somebody like her, you never feel dumb like you should have kept your stupid mouth shut. Mrs. Peggy Treadway is nothing like Mom when it comes to things. She never even tried to ride me when I'd say something that doesn't fit good into things. Mom gets good and on my case when I say something that doesn't fit into things, so like with the haircut comment Mom would ride me like there's no tomorrow for that one.

So I start cutting my hair. The scissors that the gypsy lady gave me from behind the counter aren't so sharp, so I know it's going to take a while. You can just tell these things like when scissors aren't so sharp. Some things are obvious when you know what the hell it is you're looking for. I try to start cutting with my left hand, but I can't. There isn't much I can do with my left hand considering how I'm right-handed, so I have to take my right hand out of my coat pocket. I don't want to, but I don't see too much going wrong in doing it considering I'm all alone in here. I don't leave the gun in my pocket though. I take it out when I take my hand out and look at it. I study it. It's a thing of beauty.

So I put the gun in the sink to free up my hands and grab the scissors with my good hand. You need to do what you need to do with the one hand that knows what the hell to do with things like scissors. I start cutting. It feels like I'm sawing my hair off or something. I can even feel some chunks being ripped right from the roots. But I don't care much because of it feeling good not to be so hot. I look in the sink and see that there's a lot of hair in it. The gun is almost covered. It looks good with the clumps of my hair almost covering the gun in the sink. And it feels damn good to have all that hair in the sink and not on my head anymore.

I look back in the mirror that's dry by now, but still has the marks of where I tried to wipe it clean with my hand. My hair looks like a bunch of stairs carved in it or something, but it feels good being so short. There is one spot of blood where I cut it too close, about an inch above my left ear, but it doesn't bug me too much because of it almost being dry. The good thing about your head is that it tends to dry faster than most things on your body if you happen to have a little accident. At least it's not running down my face or anything like that. You look suspicious with blood running down your face.

I grab the gun out from under my cut-off hair and blow it off. You can't have hair on your gun when you're trying to hold it tough and intimidating. So I put the thing back deep in my coat pocket, throw the hair from the sink into the toilet, and flush it. Then I rinse down the sink good and wipe the scissors off so the lady who was nice wouldn't have to clean up after me. Nobody needs to clean up after you especially in a place like a bathroom. And especially not somebody as nice as the gypsy lady.

But I can't clean up as much as I'd like to right now considering the gypsy lady might get it into her head that I've been in here too long and call somebody like the fire department to come and get me the hell out. The last thing I need is the fire department coming here and getting into my business. So I get out of the bathroom quick but cool. When I come out of the bathroom and through that skinny hallway though, the lady, well, her face just falls and I know right off the bat it's because of my hair. I don't care much because of my feeling better. I know it looks bad. But when you're hot, you're hot. Right.

I hand her the scissors and say, thank you again, remembering my manners. She takes them by the point, and I see her just staring at my head noticeable. She seems more interested in my head than in my sincere thank you. She's curious as hell. Hell, I don't know why she's looking at me so goddamn funny. I was hot. What's so funny about that. I don't tell her that her teeth are too yellow for her mouth. In fact, I don't even stare at them at all. And besides that, maybe if more people satisfied themselves when they're hot like cutting their hair off or something there might be a little more happiness around this place.

She looks at me in the face now. And let me tell you something, it's not easy for her to tear her stupid eyes away from my head. She's looking at me like I can't remember what it was that just happened in the bathroom two seconds ago. Like I can't remember, or don't really know that the hair that was there before is now gone. I remember things though. I know things like the back of my stupid hand. 25 right—15 left—4 quick right. Not everyone is so goddamn quick to recall their locker combination on the spot just like that, and then say it as easily as if they just sneezed or something.

Of course I know what the hell it was that I did in her tiny little crap hole. I cut my stupid hair off. Simple as that. I didn't play with my junk, or explode in the toilet like I wanted to do like nobody's business, or even mess one little thing up for chrissakes. I cut my hair. I was hot. And now I remember clear as a bell why it is that you don't trust people even if they do give you a nice smile. I remember all kinds of things, lady.

Anyways, then all the gypsy lady can think to ask me is why I'm not in school. I look at her for a second trying to read her face. Since she doesn't have her nice smile anymore or that nice voice either, I tell her I'm on my way just so she doesn't feel like she needs to get on my case. The one person in my whole day who I thought wouldn't get into her suspicions. Goddamnit. Shows how much I know. I don't need her in her suspicions or feel like she needs to ride me. That's the last thing I need right now from her. Mom rides me just fine all on her own. And today, well, today she's going to ride me good. She's going to know for sure that the tabs she thinks she keeps on me are all blown to hell.

CHAPTER ELEVEN

I walk out of the gypsy shop and instead of turning right to go to school like I told the lady I was going to do, I turn left and head farther into Old Town. Screw the gypsy lady. She's just like all the rest getting into her suspicions quick all because of a haircut. I don't care what I told her I was going to do. I'm not going to school. I'm going to keep on walking. I'm not even going to look back. It's only a haircut, lady. I was hot.

My walking doesn't get me very far before I stop in front of the book shop and peek at myself in the window to look at my handy work one more time. I've never been in a book shop if you want to know the way of things. Look at all those books in there. There are so many, and I know not one of them says much. Not a thing really. Who really needs to read books anyways. All they are is a bunch of smarties flexing their smartie muscle when they sit down to write a bunch of crap you don't need to know. Who needs to know what some made-up guy, or better yet what some stupid made-up girl, does for chrissakes. I'll tell you who, people with too much time on their hands, that's who. The kind of people who have nothing better to do with their time than to get into their suspicions. They all probably have a closet full of corduroy, too. I hate corduroy.

Why would I read something some smartie has to say. It's a waste of my time considering I have what I need to know already good and in my head. Not to mention all the other things that just creep in there and weigh on my mind even at night when I'm just trying to get a little shut-eye. It sure was a thing of beauty how those college kids stared at me. They just stared. They can close one of their smartie books, but they can't ignore good old Dusty Sparrow anymore. No sir. It's all about me getting in their heads good now. There's no turning their back the hell on me anymore.

All I can think on by now is Dave Treadway. I just can't shake him out of my head. So I turn away from the books, back towards the gypsy shop, and take a right on the street in between the two that I know goes up to the park. There's other streets to take to get to the park, but I take the one I know most people don't like to use. You get to know your way around a town good when you have to travel it by foot. I don't know why people don't like to use it, it's a pretty street especially now with the trees turning green and the new flowers that think now's a good time to pop their pretty little heads out.

One of those old-time street cars used to go up and down this street. The tracks are still there, but the car hasn't been on them since long before I ever came into things. Right about now I'm wishing it still did ride up and down those tracks. The shoes Mom got me with her slutty money are supposed to be good traveling shoes, but they aren't worth a crap. You don't need to worry on how your feet hurt, especially not when there's other things about the day to worry on. Like how you almost flubbed things up good back at the college. But the shoes are supposed to be the best. That's what the guy at the store said anyways. Thinking back on it though he probably would've said anything to get Mom to smile her pretty smile at him one more time. But the shoes Mom got me don't do much for comfort when you're running and walking around town. It could be worse I guess. Things can always be worse.

Besides the point that the street is pretty and it'll get me to the park, I take it because somehow I get it into my head that I might see Mr. Bones. Now not only is Dave Treadway good and in my head so is Mr. Bones. It just pops into my thinking like a burst of thunder or something that just comes out of the air from nowhere. And just like that I have to see him. No ifs, ands, or buts. I haven't seen much of him for a long time, but Mr. Bones is the kind of guy you can't keep out of your head, and it always happens just like I told you about before with it coming like thunder. It's my own fault he doesn't come around anymore. There's things I regret in life, but nothing as much as what happened with Mr. Bones.

Anyways, I know this is the street where he usually stays. I know this because of him always carrying a wore-out bag from the grocery store right on the corner here of the pretty street I'm walking on. He never goes anywhere without that bag. He carries his whole life in that one wore-out grocery store bag. He let me look in it once, and what I saw was an extra pair of red socks so he could switch when the one pair he was wearing needed to be aired out, a pack of gum that was already half-chewed, a beat-up pink comb that looked like a dog had a field day with it, and his dice.

The dice is where his name comes from. I've heard him called Mr. Bones before by all the friends he has when he wins extra cash by rolling people in the alley behind where Mom and me stay. And by rolling I mean he takes the money they put down fair and square. Everything is always on the up-and-up with Mr. Bones. What other name could he have when all he does is carry some dice around every place he goes. I know his buddies call him that because of the dice. It's a good name, too, but when I think of him being Mr. Bones, I think of his knees. When he walks it looks like there's nothing in his knees but bone. Just bone on bone crunching every time he takes a step. So that's where I got to know what to call him. He was no help when it came to knowing. Every time I'd ask his name before we got to be tight the two of us, he'd smile big and say something like, a name is just a name, and then never answer my question. But I couldn't just call him nothing, so it's been Mr. Bones from then, and it will be for a long time to come.

I know Mr. Bones doesn't have a house or anything like that because I asked him once where it was that he stayed. He told me he liked to stay in the weather. I don't worry about him, though. He knows the ins and outs about how to take care of himself. Even if he does live his whole life outside left up to good old Mother Nature. She must be good to him because of he's lived a good long life left up to that lady. Mom says God is good to people like Mr. Bones. She never said why she just said God is always good. I guess if God controls the weather like she says then I guess I can see her point.

Besides, he doesn't have to worry about staying in the weather like I'd have to worry about staying in the weather like nobody's business. If I was to decide to stay in the weather like Mr. Bones, well, first of all I'd be fried to a good and ugly crisp. You can't have ridiculous blonde hair, albino-like, and pale skin like myself and be able to stand in the sun for one minute too long. You turn a painful color of red quick. But Mr. Bones, well, Mr. Bones is a whole different thing with his dark skin. He could stand naked as a jay bird all day long, and it wouldn't make one damn bit of difference. I saw him once walking around naked as a jay bird in the back of where we stay. He was the same color all the way down to the tips of his baby toes. There was no line like I get a line from wherever it is the sun hits me where I'm not covered by my clothes. It's obvious to tell where the hell it is that my T-shirt goes. Sometimes when I'm good and naked, it looks like I have a T-shirt on anyways. But I never stay good and naked for long so nobody really ever gets to see what I'm talking about. Mr. Bones can hang out all day long in the sun, and you can't tell one little bit.

I know like there's no tomorrow that my face will be red when I wake up tomorrow morning because of my being out here in the sun all this time like I have been. Like I told you about before, spring around here is a funny thing. This morning you could see your breath plain as day in the air and now, well, now it's a whole different thing. The sun is bright and hot, too. I know when I see Mr. Bones though he'll have his coat buttoned right to the top just like myself. I know this considering I know Mr. Bones. He's either naked as a foolish jay bird or wearing every dumb thing he has. It's just the way of things when it comes to Mr. Bones.

Sometimes I'd just like to run off and stay with Mr. Bones, but then I think better of things because of my not wanting to leave Mom hanging all by her lonesome. She sure would ride me about it if I ever just didn't come home. Besides that, who'd want to walk around everyday of their life a red painful color. I don't. And it's important to think on that because of that's what living in the weather would do to somebody like me. But who knows how things would be if I didn't have Mom to think on.

Anyways, on super-cold days he used to crash in the shed in our backyard with a couple of his buddies, when there was a shed in the backyard is what I mean. It takes Mr. Bones a while to get places, but that doesn't matter much to him. When you live in the weather, you just let good old Mother Nature decide where it is your knees can take you that day. When you live in the weather you don't have to be anywhere special at any special time, so you can choose to stay wherever it is that night that'll keep you warm. Mr. Bones had a lot of buddies considering he was good with the dice, and I know they were good and happy when Mr. Bones decided to crash in our shed for the night. That way they could stay there, too, and cash in on Mr. Bones's new fortune. He was never stingy when it came to the money he won when he rolled people like Mike the sonofabitch. It'll get you all kinds of friends if you know how to share your wad of the green stuff.

Things can get good and cold around here so it's nice when you can stay in somebody's shed. It was cool of Mom letting Mr. Bones stay in the shed. I never minded him being around Mom either. He's the only guy I ever saw that didn't lose his mind when it came to Mom. Every time he stayed in the shed, he was nice and tipped his head when he'd see her. But that's it. It was never like the rest. His eyes were always clear when he looked at her. You knew as good as you know the back of your own hand there was nothing in his eyes like all those jokers. Him coming around like he did all stopped quick though when the shed burned down. Sometimes when I think on it, my stomach gets irritated like a cut you forgot to clean out good before it scabs over and has to wait around till it gets good and hard and falls off.

But the backyard is a no good place. I never go in the backyard anymore after what happened. The backyard is worse than the front. At least Mike the sonofabitch pays some attention when it comes to the front. I guess the backyard got the way it is because of it being easy to ignore something in the back that you never have to see. It looks more like a trash dumpster than a backyard. There isn't even much grass anymore. I know there used to be grass that covered all over the whole thing. How I can tell this is by all the spots of grass that are still there. You can tell they're missing all the other grass around that used to keep it company. I don't know what keeps those spots alive. Mom doesn't do one bit of anything to keep it alive. All I can figure on is the beer that gets thrown back there. Beer seems to keep most of the jokers around here alive, who's to say it doesn't do the same thing for the grass. I never go back there now considering how it's disgusting, and I only went back there when Mr. Bones was there when I was a kid because of it being no place for any kid to hang around by themself. It was scary without Mr. Bones around.

I guess I'm not being completely honest when I say I never went back there. When I said it, I meant I knew a hell of a lot better than to go back there alone. But there was this one time, there always seems to be a one time when things get messed up good, you ever notice that. But there was this one time that I had to go in the backyard. It wasn't my idea though. I knew better of things even back then. It was when I was about eight or so and Mom had a date over at the house.

I guess thinking back on it I brought the whole thing on myself. Mom made things plain as day how things were supposed to go when she had a date over, and I didn't listen. I knew that I wasn't supposed to stick my nose into Mom's business and especially not to go into that bedroom. But I remember that day I could hardly stand it, keeping to myself like I was supposed to do. The noises they were making in that bedroom, well, it was enough to make my stomach turn to hell with worry. I tried my best to play in my room like I was supposed to do, but the noises they were making kept getting louder. I thought they were hurt, considering nobody makes noises like that otherwise.

So I got concerned and went into Mom's room without knocking. I only opened it a crack so I could stick my head in, but you're always supposed to knock when it comes to Mom's room. Always. Let me tell you something, I've never forgotten it since. They were naked on the mattress on the floor. He had her folded right the hell in half like she was one of those people you hear about in the circus. So, like I told you about before, I thought they were hurt so I said, hey, not loud, but they heard me anyways. The date looked up at me and said, get out of here you goddamn kid go play in the backyard or something. Mom didn't say anything, but she stopped making those noises. I was glad about that. But that's how I landed myself in the backyard. All because the date told me to.

It was winter when the date told me to go in the back. The winter is the worst with the steps that you have to take outside the back door to get in the backyard. The ice on the steps gets to be thick and good and slippery. Good old Jack Frost doesn't mess around when it comes to those steps. Somebody could get messed up taking one wrong step on that ice, you know, snapping their neck right in two or something.

Take me, for example, most times I can walk on ice on a sidewalk or a street or something like I'm walking on air, but that ice on the back steps, well, that's a whole different thing. That ice would crack every dumb bone in my body if I tried to walk across it, so I sat down and scooted down the steps and into the backyard. I was only eight, like I said before, but I was no fool. Even at eight you know it would be bad to break your neck on some thick ice on your back steps. And besides that, I only had two choices in the matter. Either scoot down the icy steps, or stand right the hell where you are on the steps and wait until your mom comes and gets you which as far as I could tell wouldn't be any time soon. So I scooted down the steps because the ice was getting cold on my feet. Ice can get to be cold when you only have on a pair of socks.

The first thing I see laying in the yard sticking out like a sore thumb was a book of matches. They were the fancy kind of matches.

You know how you notice things quick when you know they don't belong there, well, that's the way it was with these matches. They were the kind nobody around here would have because they weren't from the gas station just up the street. I knew those matches considering I see them all the time and I had no interest in them, but the fancy ones, well, the fancy ones were a whole different thing.

They were just laying there on the ground with all the soggy leaves that used to be frozen with ice, and some bottle caps like the ones Mom used to pop off her beers when she was into beer. Mom had a real thing for beer when I was eight so the backyard was good and filled with those things. It smelled like hell in the backyard that day which didn't fit into things with it being winter. Winter is the best time of year for air around here, so it was strange. Anyways, I pick up the matches, considering they were fancy, and walked into the shed. I go in the shed considering I was cold, and the date didn't give me much chance to get my coat or shoes either for that matter.

There wasn't a door on the shed so it made it easy to look in to see if there was anything scary I needed to know about. Like what I don't know, but the last thing you want to do is happen upon something that doesn't want to be happened upon at that particular moment. I knew already that Mr. Bones and his buddies weren't in there considering it was the middle of the day. It was only on a rare day that they would sleep all the way through the middle of the day to the night. Only on a day when Mr. Bones had it good with the dice the night before and bought a bottle full of the rusty orange colored stuff for everybody to drink.

So I go in there and burn the matches. One by one. Slow. It's a miracle they weren't all wet and ruined. I guess that's what you get with the fancy matches. Miracles. I know how to light a match considering those are the kinds of things you learn when you're a kid and in the bad part of town. There's matches all over the place, and sometimes you just pick them up to have a little bit of hoot-and-holler time. But I was lighting the matches that day to try and keep the hell warm, not for fun like usual.

One gets away from me on accident and lights the whole damn shed up. I don't want to light the whole damn shed up, but it just happens. I got out before I caught fire, too, which I was glad of. I was only eight or so, but even then, I was no fool. I knew fire could mess you up bad. So I get out of there and watch the fire. I don't yell for Mom or the date considering they were doing whatever they were doing, and besides that they would try to put it out. It was a thing of beauty. Nobody should put out a thing of beauty. Besides, they would be mad as hell if they ran out and slipped on the steps breaking who knows the hell what on their body all because of me yelling.

I didn't feel so bad about the shed that day because of my already feeling bad about having to be in the backyard in the first place, but I can't hardly stand how I feel now knowing what I did to Mr. Bones. I just had to focus myself on something beautiful to get the noises Mom was making out of my head. I'm not even going to mention how I just needed a little heat to get me through. I would never do anything like that to Mr. Bones had I thought one half a second about it. But things just don't work out that way sometimes.

Anyhow, I need to stop thinking on it right now before I make my own self good and sick over what I did. I used to see some of Mr. Bones even after what I did with the matches. But I haven't seen much of him since before we moved into the nice place. I haven't seen him at all since before we moved into the nice place if I'm going to be completely honest with things. You don't get to know people like him when all you see are nice houses and the clean people who live in the nice houses. It doesn't matter much even that we're back to our own place now. When things change, they change good and forever sometimes. That seems to be the case here with what I'm talking about.

But after the day the shed burned down, Mr. Bones still came around to the alley in the back from time to time. He's a business man, and he knows that the jokers that go into the shop aren't, including Mike the sonofabitch. The jokers that go into that place, well, who knows what the hell it is that they think. But I always knew when it was that Mr. Bones was in the alley rolling people. He even taught me how to throw the dice good, and how to do it and look cool. He rolled Mike the sonofabitch more times than I can remember right in the alley behind his own foul business for chrissakes. What a business running a shop like that. I guess there's just things I'll never get.

Mr. Bones never called me by my name. Like I told you about before, he doesn't get into names. It never bothered me considering how I feel about my name in the first place. In fact, I couldn't have been happier about it. But he had a whistle that he used just for me. It was clear as a bell, and I could hear it from anywhere that I was. He didn't even use his fingers to do the whistle. He just curled his lips in and blew, and when I heard it, I ran as fast as my legs would take me to get wherever Mr. Bones was. Mom never did ride me when I went to see Mr. Bones in the alley. There's just people you know are good and Mr. Bones, well, you just know he's good. Every once in a while Mom gets things straight.

I can't say much for people in general. I don't know many people that can when I think on it. That lady in the gypsy shop was nice for a while, then all of a sudden, just like that, her nice smile went away. That's the way it happens most times. Most people are crappy deep down and get into their suspicions quick, but I can say a whole mouthful of good about Mr. Bones. There aren't a whole hell of a lot of things I can even think up for myself, but Mr. Bones, well, he's a whole different thing. No regular people even look at him sideways much less say hello to him, and the thing they don't know is the things they're missing out on. See that's what I mean about things when it comes to people. It's enough to make even a full stomach, when you're lucky enough to have one, turn to hell.

CHAPTER TWELVE

I'm at the grocery store by now, and I'm looking hard to find Mr. Bones. Like I told you about before, I have to see him no ifs, ands, or buts. I do it sly and cool, but I'm looking hard like if you were trying to find your last quarter you dropped in the grass. I don't see him right off the bat, not that I really expect to anyways, but I look hard through some of the faces around here to see if I can see where Mr. Bones is.

It's not an easy thing to do though because of Mr. Bones isn't the kind of guy you see even when you're looking extra hard for him. The thing is, you can only find Mr. Bones if he wants you to find him. Like when he used to whistle for me I knew he wanted me around. But when I went looking for him like the one day I got it in my head that he might be my dad and I wanted to ask him if he was, he was just nowhere to be found. There was no finding Mr. Bones that day. I know now that it was one of the more stupider thoughts I ever had. It's like night and day with the two of us, so there's no way he could be my dad. And besides that, I know he doesn't think of Mom in those kinds of ways. But when you're a kid, your head will do all kinds of things to make the only guy who was ever nice to you into being your dad. Your head will take you all kinds of places when you're a kid.

I'm not having much of any luck on my own trying to find Mr. Bones, so I ask this lady that is just sitting on the curb like she owns the place or something if she knows where it is that Mr. Bones is right now. She's just sitting on the curb there talking quietly not seeming to look at anything except out into the air like she's blindfolded by the clouds or something. She's rocking a little bit like she's trying to keep herself warm even though it's hot as hell right now, and she's wearing a long thick snot-green colored coat.

There's this butterfly that's weird on the coat she keeps buttoned to the top. I can't figure on why she keeps her coat buttoned to the top tight around her neck. It looks tough to breathe. But the butterfly on her coat, well, it's not a real live butterfly like you'd think. Things get too cold around here in the middle of the night for a pretty butterfly to stay alive just yet. We're a few months off from that. The butterfly is just a big decoration sewn on the left side of the jacket over her heart to make the thing pretty. Everybody wants to look nice sometimes.

She plays like she doesn't hear me and keeps talking to who the hell knows who. I clear my throat and hum a little to see if I can hear my voice, and also to see if what I asked came out of my mouth instead of just staying in my head like it likes to do sometimes. Then I say, bam, kind of loud just to practice, and then ask the same thing about knowing where Mr. Bones is. I don't understand what it is that is coming out of her mouth though considering I don't think she's saying any real kinds of words. It's a whole lot of nonsense. But I ask again because of my wanting to find Mr. Bones bad. I tell her something along the lines about my having no cash on me to give to her but that if she would help me I'd do something nice later on in the day. I mean it, too, what I'm saying to the lady. I'll do anything to find some cash for her, especially if she can help me find Mr. Bones. When you say something like that to somebody, you have to be true in what you're saying. Things don't matter much if you can't have your word be your word.

I'm trying like hell to negotiate with this butterfly lady when

I see a guy out of the corner of my seeing. He's just staring right at me like he thinks there's more to me than there really is. Like I'm walking around with three heads like some kind of monster he doesn't believe in anyhow. I don't know how old he is because of it being hard to tell somebody's age when their face has all kinds of dust and hair all over it. But he's looking at me plain as day from the parking lot way up next to the grocery store. He's just staring at me extra still.

If I had to guess on how old he is, I'd say he's about the same age as Mom. I can't see him all too good, but if I close my one eye I can see him a little better. His eyes are clear just staring at me, and if you're older like the butterfly lady is older, well, your eyes aren't that clear or the white part that white. The butterfly lady's eyes are gray and even when she's looking right the hell into your face, like she turned her head to do to me at one point, you can't tell where it is she's looking at. Her face is pointed at you, but her eyes are a whole other thing. Not to mention the part that's supposed to be white is a pale yellow. It's a color I've never seen before. If I had to guess on it though, I'd say it's like the color of mustard being mixed with milk like it happens sometimes on your plate when it's hot-dog day at school. But that's only if I had to guess on it. Hot-dog day at school is the best. You always get potato chips and a pickle on the side with your hot-dog. How I know about the mustard and how it looks is because of that's the only thing I put on my hot-dog. Mustard is the only way to go with your good and tasty hot-dog. I know what I'm talking about when I say it.

But like I told you about before, it's hard to tell on the guy who's staring at me how old he is. Not that it matters much with my purposes right now. I can't worry on him or how old he is, considering I'm trying hard to listen to what the butterfly lady is saying in case she does know something about Mr. Bones. I'm waiting for anything at all really. Anything other than the nonsense that keeps coming out of her useless mouth spraying me like somebody's sneeze you happened to walk through at the exact wrong minute. It's hard though to try to get something out of somebody that's talking crazy anyways, but to add on top of that somebody else that's staring you down extra still from the parking lot, well, your nerves get shot quick. I'm just wishing like hell he'd stop looking at me. Life is hard enough to get through without people staring you down good. Especially somebody like him that seems to know things about you that you don't even know about your own self.

I don't know what's so interesting to him anyways. I'm just standing here trying to talk to the butterfly lady about something that's good and important for chrissakes. I'm not doing anything, not one little stupid thing. I try my best to keep on ignoring the guy, but it's hard to ignore something that you can feel all the way in your stomach and know like there's no tomorrow that the guy staring you down in the parking lot knows what you're all about. It's like I'm standing here naked as a jay bird. Hell, I feel like this guy is turning me inside out and looking at my insides like one of those diggers who looks for dinosaur bones or something.

I can't take the guy looking at me anymore, and I tell the butterfly lady to hold on a minute so I can ask the guy what the hell is so interesting. She doesn't hold on a minute, she just keeps right on talking her nonsense. But I look up anyways and just like that, like it was something I made up in my head or something, the guy is just gone. People don't just vanish like that, I don't care who you are. I'm weirded out by now and want to get the hell out of here quick. I can tell the butterfly lady isn't going to say a thing that's worth my time anyways, so I start heading to the park like I was doing in the first place before my head started working overtime. She keeps talking to the air like she has been since I stopped, but all of a sudden, she tells me to pray to Jesus. Right to my back, when I'm almost out of earshot, she gets her tongue in order and says something like that to me. I turn quick and ask her if I need to pray to Jesus for Mr. Bones. She just looks at me quiet but steady not giving me much of anything to go on. I say thanks and start walking again leaving her to her business. Cut your losses and go on.

I know there are more people that are hidden right now that I could ask on where it is that I could find Mr. Bones, but I think better of things. If that lady meant what she said about praying to Jesus, well, there's just things I'd rather not know about today, and that's one of them. When you start poking around asking all kinds of questions, sooner or later you're going to get some answers, and they might be exactly what you didn't want to hear. Besides that, I don't want to try my luck with the guy who just vanished, just like that he's gone into thin air.

So I pass the grocery store on the corner, cross a street it doesn't look like too many cars use, and keep on my merry way walking to the park. That's where I was headed in the first place before I got it into my head that I needed to see Mr. Bones. Mr. Bones doesn't even like somebody that messes with guns or even knives for that matter. I don't know what I was thinking. Sometimes what your own head can do to you, well, it takes a lot out of you. Today is all about the prospects. Dave Treadway will know what the hell it is I'm trying to get at. I don't know why I got caught on seeing Mr. Bones anyways. It's Dave who I need to be looking for right now. See what I'm saying about your own head sometimes.

CHAPTER THIRTEEN

So I'm walking to the park trying to forget my mistake in going to the grocery store. It takes me a little while to get there, but when I do get there, far from my mistake, my head's pretty clear, so I decide to walk through the middle of the park. I walk right down the middle because of my liking it here so much and thinking it's pretty. I don't have to walk through the park to get to where I'm going. I can just stay on the streets, but I want to see its beauty considering I don't get to the park much anymore. It's quite a hike from where we stay, so most times I just try to stick close to home. It sure is pretty though. Everybody needs a change of pace every once in a while.

How pretty it is makes me feel a little bad about what I did, you know with the college kids, even though it didn't quite go as planned. But I get over it quick. Sometimes things in your life need to be shaken a little and told to wake the hell up and pay attention to how good you have it. Of course, I'm talking about those college kids and not myself. I know which way is up. But all that kind of seems to vanish in the trees right now. Like I said, I get over it quick. The park is a nice place, and I need to appreciate that it's a nice place to be. Especially right now with the situation being as it is with it being spring around here. The trees are tall, and the leaves are just starting to grow again. I don't know how they make it through the mornings considering it's super-cold in the mornings this time of year. But they make it through, and I'm glad. They're super-nice to look at.

Anyways, I get here, and Dave Treadway is still in my head. I know my intentions here are to find him, but you can't come to a beautiful place and not take the time to appreciate it, you know stopping and smelling the roses and that crap. But Dave was cool with those kinds of things, too. He knew everything about everything. He knew how to fight good and talk tough, but then he also knew the names of all the trees and flowers around the park. Let me tell you something, there's a lot of trees and flowers around the park and Dave knew all the names good. He was smart, that guy. It didn't matter much to him that I'm not super-smart. We were just cool, the two of us. He liked telling me things he knew, and I liked hearing them.

He taught me a lot of things. Like this one time he showed me how to dip. He looked cool doing it, good and tough, so I did it. I hated it, but even after that if Dave took a dip and offered me one, I always took it. Dave Treadway is not the guy you turn down. Not if you want to look cool, that is. I guess it didn't matter how many times I had to puke in the toilet or right the hell in the trees for that matter when it came to taking a dip with Dave. No matter how many times I exploded out of my face all kinds of nasty colored chunks, I still packed a fat one. When you have a friend like Dave Treadway in your corner, you do what you have to do to keep him there.

Like to show you what I'm talking about here. From where he came from before, somewhere in California but I don't know what city, he wrestled at his high school. He said he couldn't wait to get on the wrestling team at the high school here in Fort Harmony. He showed me some moves once or twice, and he was good. Not that I really knew the difference between being good and being bad. I couldn't have really given a goddamn about the whole thing. I couldn't even hold my own when it came down to it, but I think Dave just wanted to beat the crap out of me anyways just for fun.

We had to take off our shirts because of Dave saying they get in the way when you're trying to wrestle. I took my shirt off even though naked makes me sick. I was just doing what I had to do to keep Dave around. Besides, how do you tell another guy that naked makes you sick. You don't. You just stand there trying to hunch in on yourself covering whatever it is you want to cover. Like your scrawny chicken chest you'd rather keep to yourself. Besides your chest, you want to cover your skinny as hell arms when the guy you're hanging around with has extra big arms. They were good and cut like a real man's would be. He was tan, too. You know the kind of tan that looks like he tried hard to get it. But Dave's not like that. He just looks that way just because.

I certainly didn't look down at my own pale thin body. Not even once. Who wants to look down and see that they're half-naked as a jay bird when naked makes them sick anyways. I'm not even going to mention being next to somebody like Dave Treadway. It was easier to wrestle around playing like I looked the way Dave did. It took a lot of my imagining to do it, but you do what you have to do sometimes to keep your friend around in your stupid life. And if your friend wants to hang out with you half-naked and just wants to beat the crap out of you, that's just what you do.

Dave was a solid guy. Noble in a Fort Harmony sort of way. He still is but I don't like to think about it because of him catching a thing for Mom. Nothing ever happened between Mom and Dave. Mom's not evil like some people are evil. I know what you're thinking to yourself. But she tries hard to ride me about the things she's supposed to. Sometimes she does good, and sometimes she misses the point. In fact, sometimes she's way the hell off mark. But that's Mom for you. She tries hard considering she's all on her own. She gives me money to buy lunches at school most times. That counts for something. And she didn't do anything with my friend. That would have been an act of evil for sure. But after that, with Dave catching a thing for Mom, the line was drawn in the sand. Everybody needs to learn when to say when, even if it means losing a friend like Dave Treadway.

But let's get back to the beginning of how things came to be with me and Dave getting to be tight, the two of us. That part I told you before about Dave being cool because of him being friends with me besides my being from the bad part of town, well, I stretched the truth some. Sometimes it happens. Like I told you before, we lived in that nice place for a while. Right by the park. Extra nice places always seem to be right by a park. I guess that's just the way of things. In the good part of town, you get parks. In the bad part of town, you get shops like the one next to where I stay and places to buy as many lottery tickets as your little mitts will hold. I guess there's a balance in there somewhere that I'm just missing right at this minute.

But the place we stayed in the good part of town was clean and kind of fancy because of the joker who owned it had a lot of money. I'm assuming he got it from some sort of upstanding job somewhere in Old Town where he goes everyday to bring home that big fat nine-to-five paycheck. But you know what they say when you assume something. He sure is a responsible nine-to-fiver that guy. I never figured out what he did at his job. Not that I cared too much to find out anyhow. Just looking at him in his khaki pants and button-down shirts and ties were enough to make me not really want to know. So I didn't give him too much of my attention. His daughter, Mindy, well, there's a whole other story for you. One that I really don't want to get into much.

It was wrong to move into that nice place like we did though. The old lady of the house had just died from some kind of cancer. Right before we moved in, she just died. As far as I can tell, the lady of the house just up and died from something that God was mean enough to give her. Cancer. Now there's a nasty thing for you. Cancer. Even the word weirds me out. Nobody, I don't care who you are, deserves what God can give them when he's having a bad day. Unless you're a real filthy bastard, you don't wish that on anybody. But Mom just moved in, you know, taking advantage of opportunity like she does, without giving two thoughts to the situation.

There I go again getting way the hell off the point. I hate when I do that. But it's easy to do when you're thinking about the times when you had it good even if it was at somebody else's expense. Anyways, I met Dave when we lived in the good part of town. His family moved to Fort Harmony when it was summer. It's a nice place in the summer. We were good and tight almost from the very second he moved in. I had just moved in myself, so it was new for the both of us.

He didn't like to stay at home much considering his dad's mean. Who could blame the guy. Nobody wants to hang out with an old man who is a nasty bastard. Besides that, what the hell did I have to stick around the house for. There's only so many times you can take feeling like hell because you're living somewhere you shouldn't be living, so Dave and me hung out at the park most times. It was convenient for the both of us. It was a good time of year, too, with it being summer in Fort Harmony. It's quiet because of those college kids going back to wherever the hell it is they came from in the first place. I wish they'd just stay there, too. There's no two ways about it. It sure was a time of beauty, that summer.

Anyways, he moved into a house close to the nice place we stayed. He didn't know a thing about me. Or Mom either for that matter so it was easy for me to play like we were regular people. Well, until I opened my big dumb mouth about us, about where Mom worked, and where we used to live. One day it just slipped out like when you think you sneeze clean and you realize you did a whole lot more than just let a little air fly. It happens to the best of us. But with this situation here, I should have just hunkered down good and kept my mouth shut tight. You're supposed to be able to feel these situations out good before they happen. Stupid me. Who's to say Dave would've caught a thing for Mom if I hadn't opened my big stupid mouth. We could still be good and tight right now if it wasn't for me.

I start looking around the park. I do it out of habit like when you look at your nails twenty times a day to see if they've grown too much from the last time you've checked, and I see his house, the Treadway household, over across from the lake. I don't know what it is I'm looking around for when I'm doing it, but when I see his house, I know that's what it was that got into my head. It's a real deal classy sort of house. You just know the people that live there have some serious cash. I almost forgot how nice this place is because of my not coming up here anymore.

I know Dave is at school considering it's the middle of the morning, I'm no fool you know, but I can't help myself from walking over to his house. So I hike it over there. It's like I don't have a choice to just stay where the hell I am and look at the tall pretty trees like I was and minding my own business. Something is keeping me moving the hell forward though like if a big wind came and picked your feet up and moved you somewhere else. I want to show him the gun and how I hold it to make me look tough and intimidating. I can't even hardly stomach the guy anymore, but he's the one I want to see right at this particular moment. Your head will do all kinds of funny things to you sometimes.

There's a lot of trees and bushes and crap in front of the windows of his house, so I have to get close to look in. I know he's not there, but I decide to look in the windows for him anyways. I look in there all noticeable with this ridiculous blonde hair shining in the shade like a light bulb. So quick I decide the best place to be is to hide in the bushes. The neighbors around here are super likely to get right the hell into their suspicions. People around here are known for getting into their suspicions. The last thing I need right now is the police or something getting on my case. Who needs the police on their case with a gun in their pocket. Things would get ugly fast, that's for goddamn sure.

So I am going to lay low in the bushes. It's not so hard to do because of the bushes smell good with the flowers on them. It makes me remember the good things about today. Today is the day Dusty Sparrow won, and I don't need anybody wrecking it for me. And besides that, I know it's a Wednesday, so the smell of the pretty flowers isn't going to be shot to hell anytime soon with the air from the slaughter town. Sometimes you just need to sit back and enjoy a good moment. Right now I can't think of a better one. I have my prospects all nestled in tight in my pocket, and I'm enjoying the hell out of some pretty flowers. Beautiful.

Dave Treadway would know exactly what it is I'm talking about. He'd especially know all the things of beauty that come with the gun I found in my own yard. Just like he would say to me if he was here, it means all sorts of good things when you find a nice gun in the leaves of your own yard Dusty old boy. Not that this one is nice, but you do with what you have most times. You need to appreciate things that come at you like they fell right out of the big blue sky.

I appreciate the hell out of my good fortune with my finding the gun. Sometimes it happens that I can't help from pulling the thing out right in the middle of the day from my coat pocket and appreciate it good. Like sometimes I wind up in the bathroom, any bathroom where I happen to be at that moment, I'm not particular when it comes to these things, and I'd hold the thing in my palm like it was a million dollars. If I thought much about how it was I got into the bathroom I could never really remember exactly how the hell it was that I got there in the first place. It's scary when you're someplace, and you don't know how you got there. But I wouldn't sidetrack myself trying to worry on it. I'd hold the gun soft in my hands like it was a tiny baby rabbit or something. When you're holding a rabbit, you always hold it soft unless you're a nasty bastard like some of the people you hear about on TV. When your TV's working, and you can hear about it, that is.

But the gun was like my little million dollar rabbit. Like this one time I went into the bathroom at my stupid school. It was dark in there. Sometimes when you get something in your head to get excited about, you forget to do stuff like turn the light on. It didn't matter much though because of feeling it was just as good, maybe even a little better, as seeing it. But right now, there's no way I could look at it even if I wanted to. You need to be smart about things like keeping your gun right the hell where it is and not be tempted to bring it out into the open in front of all kinds of people who get into their suspicions quick. Never mind that you are sitting here hidden in the bushes, people that get into their suspicions can see right through walls if that's what they have to do to get what they want to know. But my hand is good and wrapped around the thing. Don't you worry about that.

CHAPTER FOURTEEN

When you're hiding in the bushes in front of the Treadway household and rubbing the gun in your pocket, all you have to do is happen to look to your left and, bam, there it is. There's the nice place where Mom and me stayed. I look over half because I mean to just for kicks and half because I have to like I can't control my eyes or something. When I thought about seeing it again I thought it might hurt to look, but it doesn't. In fact, I'm not feeling much of anything about it right at the minute. It sure is a nice place, and regular when you're looking from the outside.

Thinking on it now, while I'm looking smack-dab right in the face of the place we used to stay, I can know like there's no tomorrow that there must've been a gun under that roof. There was a gun right under my stupid nose the whole time, and it's taken me till now to know it. It hits me right between the eyes like a stupid two-by-four. I'm no fool, so how I missed it, well, shame on me. Shame the hell on stupid me. I can't help you, pal, if you don't pick up on clues that are spelled right out for you. Sometimes you just need to wake the hell up and learn how to be smart about things. Smell the goddamn coffee once in a while.

So how I come to know this while I'm sitting here in the bushes being still like a statue is because of my good memory I was telling you about before. It's a freaky thing how things come back to you when you are looking smack-dab right in the face of them and where it is that they happened. The stuff about the gun was spelled out for me right to my face by the girl who actually belonged living in the place. It was spelled out like a stupid neon sign for chrissakes. I'm remembering plain as day how she told me that she'd blow my big nose off if I didn't leave her alone. I can't figure on why she said that to me, about my having a big nose. My nose is a normal-sized nose. Now Jackson the nine-to-fiver has a super-big nose with a big ass bump on it. You know the kind of bump that he probably has to see even when he's looking straight the hell ahead. But my nose, well, I can't see my nose unless I look down at it. If you don't have a big nose, you get good and cross-eyed when you look down and try to see it.

I probably scared the girl a big one if I want to admit to the truth of things. I didn't want to scare her, but that's what must've happened. Dave was always putting it in my head that I should do stuff with her. You know, naked stuff. Like I told you about before, naked makes me sick but Dave, well, he started riding me about it. He'd start asking me every time I saw him if I'd done anything to that nice tail yet. He was always talking to me saying stuff like, your sister's got a nice tail Dusty boy, and stuff like, what I wouldn't do with a nice tail like that. She wasn't my sister, and Dave knew that, but he was always saying it for reasons I don't know. You don't ask Dave his reasons on things even if it does get good and under your skin. You just tell yourself he must have some.

On more than one occasion, he told me things about girls and how to make them squirm like a little pig right under you. He said to never underestimate the power of a touch on a girl who squirms like a pig, that's what he called it, too, the power of a touch. Who talks like that. But he told me how to get a girl in the sack fast but smooth. I listened considering you don't not listen to Dave. He seemed to know what he was talking about, but I couldn't give a crap.

Dave told me stuff on how to get Mindy to squirm like a little pig. He told me to pay attention and snapped his fingers in my face like a real asshole to make good and sure I hung on every word he said. So I did. I looked him hard in the eyes when he told me stuff I didn't care one little bit about. He said, you gotta get drunk on the good stuff to do it though, none of that crap that runs right through you and makes your head feel like a ten gallon tank. He was sure that you had to get drunk. I never bothered to tell him I knew a whole lot of things about that naked stuff because of my being behind the counter at the shop all the time. It's enough of that kind of stuff in my head to last a lifetime.

What he was saying must've gotten good and in my head one night though. I'm not proud of it, but it's what happened. It turned me into being almost like one of those jokers at the shop. I'm not super-clear on what it was that I was doing to the girl, Mindy is who I'm talking about, when she kept saying, would you stop it, and, get off me you smelly freak. It can't be too much of anything serious because she had her clothes on good and closed and tucked in and everything else. And me, well, I had my clothes good and on including my damn shoes. And on top of everything else, I had my hands in my pockets. You can't do much of anything with your hands shoved all the way down to the lint-filled bottoms of your pockets. But I must've rolled on top of her somehow considering how else would she need to be pushing me up off of her. It must've been good and hard to get me the hell off, too. Your face doesn't just get that red unless you're trying extra hard at something like getting somebody off you like you think if you don't you're going to die or something. I must've weighed a whole hell of a lot at the time, too, with my hands in my pockets with not an ounce of supporting myself.

Anyways, she told me she'd blow my big nose off, and I knew she meant it. When somebody's face is already red, so red it's close to being an ugly as all get out purple, and then gets all shaky and their voice gets deep, you know they mean business. And Mindy meant some business. Shame on me for not putting two and two together about that gun. Things might've gotten good for me a long time ago had I known to put two and goddamn two together. I'm kicking myself good here in the bushes for missing that one.

Jackson the nine-to-fiver was no slouch, so I know like there's no tomorrow that he'd pack one hell of a nice gun. It would be shiny and smooth. It would work, too, because of you don't spend a wad of cash like I know Jackson the nine-to-fiver had on some piece of crap that didn't even work. If I only knew. It makes me so sick right now I could vomit. But I can't think on it. I need to steady my head and think on my own situation right now. The prospects are alive and well today. I'm not going to let my stupid head mess things up just because I couldn't see the writing on the wall. Always look at the prospects you have right at that moment in your life. God bless America for the prospects. Amen.

CHAPTER FIFTEEN

While we stayed there, in the nice place is still what I'm talking about, Mom quit the shop and told Mike the sonofabitch to go to hell. I know it was the thought of being a sort of family is what got Mom all tingly in her stomach when she told Mike the sonofabitch to go to hell. Now we all know she got way ahead of herself on that one, but that's a whole other thing for a whole other time.

When you want to get right down to it, Mom and me, well, we're basically orphans out here in Colorado. She obviously wanted it that way, leaving Boston like she did, but it doesn't change the facts that being alone is being alone. And in this case here, I'm more alone than Mom is because of my not even having anybody in my head that I can know and know they are parts of my blood. I'm not even going to count that short bastard, so there's nobody. Well, except for Mom that is. Of course there's always Mom, and you can never forget about her.

I know there's at least one brother of Mom's back there in Boston because of my hearing what Mom said once to Mike the sonofabitch about him doing something just like her goddamn brother. Just like that, that's what she said, her goddamn brother. I don't know what the hell Mike the sonofabitch could do that would be anything like somebody that has the same blood as me would do. Most guys wouldn't piss in the same pot as Mike the sonofabitch much less do something like him. And someone from my own blood. That's just something I can't quite swallow. I'd never be caught dead doing anything like Mike the sonofabitch. Hell, I'd run around naked as a jay bird before I'd do anything like him, and we all know how I feel about naked. It makes me sick.

Anyways, ever since I heard her say that to Mike the sonofabitch, I've been curious. It's easy to get into your suspicions when somebody mentions somebody else you never heard of before and they're related to you. I never asked Mom about it considering she gets all worked up and tells me her business is her business, and then runs for the stupid stash of tissues and rosary beads when I do. It's only happened once or twice. You learn your lesson quick in situations like these. Nobody likes to make anybody run for their box of tissues and rosary beads.

But this brother of hers, well, I've given him a name because of my liking to think of him with a name. Bobby O'Malley. It has a nice ring to it. Most times I wish that it was my name instead of Dusty Sparrow. It sounds good with my face. My face was meant for a name like Bobby O'Malley. You know how people would talk saying things like, wow there goes that Bobby O'Malley, like when I'd walk down the hall at school. Like I told you before though, it's a name I made up, but it fits in my head. The way Mom said that to Mike the sonofabitch, all insulting like he's probably tough and cool as hell, has to be about somebody with a name like Bobby O'Malley.

But Mom tried hard to forget about her family back in Boston. It's not that she was against families in general, not like she wanted to be an orphan. Look at how she got so excited when the opportunity with this rich joker came along. She saw a prime opportunity when the guy came in the shop looking for something just after his wife died, things I just don't get and hope I never get. In some ways, you have to feel a little bad for the guy being lonely like he was and not knowing what the hell to do with himself. But in all the other ways all you want to say right to the guy's face is, perk your better senses the hell up and know when you're doing a disgusting and wrong sort of thing. I can't imagine her body was even cold when Mom decided to pounce like she likes to do. She's always saying that when an opportunity comes along, you've got to grab it by the balls and hang on good and strong. It's best not to think too hard on things Mom says most times though. Trust me. I'm telling you the God's honest truth.

When I think on it I can't imagine why it is that Jackson the nine-to-fiver ever let Mom and me step one foot into that nice place. The nine-to-fiver Jackson seemed like a smart kind of a guy, like he had his head screwed on straight, so I can't figure on why such a smart guy would think it was even half of a good idea for us, Mom and me, to move in like we did. It was obvious from the start that the girl who actually belonged living in the place, Mindy, didn't want to have anything to do with anything that involved me and Mom. I can't blame her really because of us being rough trade and putting a damper on her nice place. But the nine-to-fiver Jackson sure lost his head when it came to that one. He must've caught a thing for Mom bad like he got the wind knocked out of him or something, and by the time he got it back, the floozy from the shop and her kid were living right the hell under his roof.

Like I told you about before a lot of guys catch a thing when it comes to Mom, but most seem to lose it just as fast, which is smart on their part because of them being able to avoid a sticky situation. But Jackson the nine-to-fiver, well, there's a guy you need to pity. Pity is an ugly thing, but here, well, here it's exactly what's called for. He didn't even see it coming and then, bam, just like that he knew like there's no tomorrow that he made a bad mistake. You need to be careful when it comes to Mom considering she works fast and quick.

It was nice for me staying in the nice place for a while, I'm no fool when it comes to knowing that one. It was nice for me, so I tried not to think too much on the crappy situation Jackson the nine-to-fiver put himself in. Thinking back on it now though makes my stomach turn to hell. The things Mom does to people is terrible most times. She doesn't even seem to see that though. What's ever good for Mom is good for Mom. That's it. End of story. There would be a lot more happiness around this place if people would just be a little nicer to other people. Is that so much to ask. But that's Mom for you, always thinking the opposite to the way of things.

She played good at being an upstanding citizen with her stupid knight in shining armor, the nine-to-fiver Jackson, who rescued her from the shop, but I know not before taking her to the counter like a responsible consumer. You know, testing the merchandise and that kind of crap. Mom got a thrill out of saying his name out loud all the time around the house because of it sounding rich. Nothing like my name. Who names their kid Dusty Sparrow for chrissakes. It sounds like I'm a filthy rotten bird or something.

Anyways, Mom played good at being an upstanding citizen for a while. I could tell she was just acting like if she finally did make it to Hollywood like she wanted to a long time ago. She did good at making it seem like she really is worth a damn and just caught an unlucky break from life. It's easy and believable when you have a pretty face like Mom does. People want to believe somebody that looks like an angel really is an angel.

She played it nice drinking hot tea and painting her fingernails red and calling Mindy all kinds of crap like sweetheart and honey and flower. Who calls anybody flower for chrissakes. I know it made Mindy's skin crawl good and like if a spider crawled in your ear or something and decided to hang out for a while. But Mom looked like the regular saints she prays to all the time, and Mindy just had to sit there shut up because of her knowing anything she said wouldn't do one bit of good anyhow. It's just the way of things when it comes to Mom.

Mom cleaned up nice, too. It doesn't take a lot of work when you already look the way Mom does. She took showers everyday, too, just like I did, and I know she liked the hot water as much as myself. Everyday her hair was clean and smelled pretty like the way Candy Carmichael's hair smells in Mr. Robbins's class. I used the shampoo that smelled good for a while but went back to bar soap because of my not wanting to turn into one of those dainty guys. Who wants to be a dainty guy. I don't. I'd shower in the dark at the nice place. Like I told you about before, naked makes me sick and, well, when it comes to the shower you can't be anything but good and naked.

Besides that, I liked it dark in the bathroom because of my being just as glad not seeing the pink-flowered wallpaper the lady who had cancer must've put up forever ago. It makes you feel bad seeing something that somebody that's now dead did while they were alive. It puts a whole new twist to things. Mom said everyday that she was going to tear it down, but Jackson cried like a baby every time she said it. But that's Mom for you, getting a kick out of watching a grown man cry like a baby over his wife that died. She's always getting a big kick out of the wrong things that make you feel like hell for just having to think on them.

But anyways, Mom looked pretty in all the things the nine-to-fiver Jackson bought for her with his big nine-to-five paycheck. As far as I go, well, that big nine-to-five paycheck bought me a couple of new T-shirts, but that's about it. I know Jackson the nine-to-fiver bought the white T-shirts to get me the hell out of the tie-dye ones he said were a goddamn embarrassment in his neighborhood.

He had a real thing against those hippie guys that made my T-shirts. He'd run his mouth sometimes, before he bought me the white T-shirts and finally shut the hell up about the whole thing, saying things like, those no good hippies don't know their asshole from the joint they put in their traps and smoke. I don't know anything about anything they would smoke, but they're OK as far as I go. I never said much when it was that I went in the place. They always said, hey, they said it just like that, too, hey, and let me go about my business picking my own T-shirts. They know when your business is your business. They'd say things about Mom every now and again like I told you about before, but even that wasn't super bad. I've seen a lot worse, like the way Dave Treadway was when it came to Mom.

I can't blame Jackson the nine-to-fiver really about what he thought about the tie-dye T-shirts. He just doesn't know the way of things when you have to wear whatever the hell it is you have to put on. You can't really blame the guy for things he doesn't know about. I didn't let what he said bug me because of my preferring the T-shirts being white and not tie-dye anyhow. I was never too crazy about the tie-dye. And I was just as glad keeping to the T-shirts because of my being used to the way I dress. Simple. No surprises. You try to put me in those khaki pants and a shirt that buttons down, and I'll run like my hair's caught on fire. I was just glad they were still the T-shirts I like to wear. But all that ended along with everything else with the nice place because of Jackson the nine-to-fiver probably finding out the true things about Mom.

For some reason, reasons I don't even know, the nine-to-fiver Jackson told Mom and me to get the hell out and never come back. He probably smartened up and realized what he got himself into. It wasn't my fault that we got kicked out of the nice place by the park. Sometimes things happen when Mom's around. Unavoidable kinds of things. I don't know what she did but it must've been good and rotten. I can't imagine what could be worse than the pink-flowered wallpaper in the bathroom and what Mom said about it, but then again, I'm not Mom.

We didn't last long in the nice place. Who expected that we would. Mom held on to her new life by her teeth though. She dragged the whole thing out for the summer. The whole damn summer. But when summer was over so was the nice neighborhood. Mom likes to pin it on me, about us being kicked out of the nice place. She's always pinning things on me that don't have much of anything about anything with me in it. Like this one time, she tried to tell Mike the sonofabitch that I was the one who took the money out of the cash register the day that it was short of its slutty money. I know that the sonofabitch Mike would have probably given it to Mom anyways considering the way he looks at her if she had just asked. If she had just said something like, hey Mike the sonofabitch I'm a little short this month, or, hey Mike the sonofabitch how about a loan. But she just found it easier to blame it on me. I took it too because of when your mom pins something on you, you don't argue. Things can get ugly quick.

I know like there's no tomorrow she took the money to buy extra lottery tickets that week. It was a big week for the lottery. You always remember when it's a big week for the lottery when you live in the bad part of town. Mom isn't even smart about it. You don't tell Mike the sonofabitch that your kid, who wasn't supposed to be in the shop in the first place, took money from the cash register. You pin it on one of the jokers that come into the place for chrissakes. Everybody knows not one of them is worth a damn as a person anyways. Who knows what the hell it is that goes on in Mom's head.

It was the same thing with Jackson the nine-to-fiver. I know like nobody's business that Mom was the one who messed that one up good and not me. But like I said before, when your mom tells you that you messed a good thing up and pins everything the hell on you, it's hard to know you didn't when that's what your mom says. Mom still likes to ride me about us having to leave the nice place. She still gets good and on my case about her having to crawl on her filthy hands and knees back to Mike the sonofabitch to get her job and the crappy shack back.

I know it wasn't as hard as Mom said considering I know Mike the sonofabitch caught a thing for Mom way before she told him to go to hell. And when a guy catches a thing for Mom, well, there's no turning back. I can probably count on one hand the things that guy wouldn't do for Mom. I know one of them is he wouldn't let Mom get on that train that goes through the middle of town, or get on a bus to get the hell out of here to someplace like Hollywood. Besides that, it's not so hard just to move right back into the bad part of town. Regular people would never live where we live. Hell, I wouldn't live where we live if it was up to me.

CHAPTER SIXTEEN

Anyways, I get those things out of my head considering the past is the past, and the last thing you want to do is live it twice. There's just some things that can be enough the first time around. So I'm in the bushes in front of the Treadway household like I told you about before I got way the hell off track. The bushes are bellied right up to the outside of the house, so I'm in good and close. If I want to look in the window all I have to do is stand up, not all the way but a little, to see right into the living room. That's a funny thing about the nice part of town. The houses here have all kinds of rooms, and I know there's no way that they can all be used. Like this living room in the Treadway household. I know it only gets used when Mr. Treadway has some of his business people over to talk about what the hell I don't know what of. Other than that it's off limits. I guess with all that white furniture you do what you have to do to keep it that way.

So anyhow, now I'm looking in the window of Dave's house like a stupid peeping Tom or something to see if he's anywhere around. I don't see Dave but I see Mr. Treadway walk into the living room right where I'm looking. I almost crap myself first of all because I see him and second of all because he looks out the window right at me for chrissakes. I hold super still because, like I told you before, he's mean and you don't want to do anything to set him off. But I guess he doesn't see me because of my being hidden in the bushes good. They're right next to the house so I think he's going to see me no problem, but the bushes are good and thick so I can stay invisible like I want to be right at this minute.

What I can't figure out is it's the middle of the morning and Mr. Treadway isn't at work. He's dressed nice in his fancy suit like he should be a work, but he's at home, and it's the middle of the morning. I know he's supposed to be some smart computer guy at some desk somewhere way the hell on the other side of town, so I know like nobody's business he has no business being at home.

He's walking across the living room cool like he does without much trying to be cool. I half expect some other guys in super-nice suits to walk in behind him, but I find out quick that that's just not the case. It's just him and that's it. He's walking cool but quick, and in a half a second, I know exactly where it is he's walking to. He's going to the booze cart thing and getting out one of those stubby little glasses to fill with the pricey stuff that gets you good and smashed, so I'm glad I'm hidden here in the bushes. Even from out here I can see that he pours himself a stiff one and takes a big drink. He doesn't even flinch, and I know it's disgusting. I know it tastes like hell. Dave and myself took a couple of pulls off Mr. Treadway's stash once. It tasted like hell. We got smashed, tanked to be exact, and between the two of us, we didn't drink half of what Mr. Treadway does. How can the guy not flinch with it tasting like hell. I know it tastes like hell water as sure as I'm sitting here.

But he sure is dressed nice. Just one time I'd like to look sharp in a suit the way Mr. Treadway does. There are some people who don't look good no matter what they're wearing, but Mr. Treadway can wear a suit and look extra good. I know I'd look good if I could wear a suit like that just once. I'd walk all over this stupid town just so people could see me looking like an upstanding citizen. If I had a suit like that I'd have to have a wad of cash in my pocket, too. You can't wear a sharp black suit around and not have a wad of cash in your pocket.

What I'd do with that wad of cash is simple. I'd walk up to somebody in one of those nice cars I was telling you about before and hold out the wad of cash and say something smooth like, how about a trade. They'd step out and I'd get in. Of course I'd smell nice in my nice suit. The first thing I'd do is I would roll down the window, turn on some music, and get way the hell out of Fort Harmony. It would be the perfect getaway car, too, you know, with everything running, and it would take me wherever the hell it is I'd want to go. Someplace like Boston or California. Someplace where I could walk on the street in my suit, even the busiest street in town, and nobody knows one little thing about me. Mr. Treadway here is dressed in his nice suit and clean-as-a-whistle white shirt and nice tie, but all he's doing is drinking the stuff that puts fire in your ass out of those stubby little glasses. He should be out walking around showing the world what he's made of. It makes you wonder sometimes when things like this are happening. Especially when they're happening right in front of your own eyes.

Anyways, he drinks down three of those stubby little glasses, and I know he has to be feeling it by now. He starts talking at himself loud. I can't understand what it is he's saying, but I can hear his voice clear as a bell like he's standing right next to me for chrissakes. He throws some nice stuff around. Expensive stuff. He does it and gets a hell of a kick out of it. He's just picking up whatever and hucking it way the hell across the room. Who wants to throw nice stuff around. I'd know better than to do a thing like that. That's for damn sure.

All of a sudden, just like when you forgot your own birthday or something and then remember it just like if a rock came and hit you in your stupid head, I think of Mrs. Peggy Treadway. I'm hoping hard that she's nowhere to be found in the house. Dainty people like Mrs. Peggy Treadway just need to be way the hell away from situations like this one here. People like Mrs. Peggy Treadway just need to put on their nice pearls and get the hell out of the house quick when Mr. Treadway starts his drinking the pricey stuff as you can see from what's going on here.

So I get freaked out by now. I'm worrying good and hard about Mrs. Peggy Treadway when I get to thinking it's only a matter of time before he looks out the window again and sees me. Things would get all kinds of ugly if he did. Sure I have the gun right in my pocket, but that kind of crap doesn't go over with Mr. Treadway. It was a dumb idea coming here in the first place because of my knowing about Dave not being here anyhow. It's the middle of the stupid morning. I should've known better than to think the guy would ever miss an opportunity like school to get out of the house. So finally, just like if God knew the mess I could end up in and decided to help me out for once, Mr. Treadway turns his back to me and throws around some more nice stuff at the other wall. Without wasting too much time with things and trying my already crappy luck, I get the hell out of the bushes fast. Fast and quiet. The last thing you want to do is jolt Mr. Treadway back to earth after he's had three of those stubby little glasses.

I stop for a half a second though when I'm about two steps from being in the clear. If Mrs. Peggy Treadway was in the house, I would have to go in there no matter how much I didn't want to and keep Mr. Treadway the hell away from her. He might not even want to hurt her, but if she even stepped one toe or one little hair on her head, in the way of the things Mr. Treadway was doing to blow off some steam, she would get hurt bad. The size of that guy is enough to knock down a whole wall if he wanted to.

Nobody wants somebody like Mrs. Peggy Treadway in the middle of something like that. But I talk myself into believing that she has to be somewhere the hell out of the house. She has to know better than to stick around when things get out of control. I have to believe it or otherwise I might not be able to stand myself that I didn't stay to keep Mr. Treadway from riding her. You always have to look out for people like Mrs. Peggy Treadway.

CHAPTER SEVENTEEN

I start heading back, running would be a better way to put it, through the park, but in the opposite direction this time. You can't run through a place where you just walked like you had nothing on your mind and then run like a bat out of hell to get out of there fast. That's when the trouble starts. But I start running fast in the opposite direction to get through the park quick because of my knowing it's only a matter of about a half a second with these people around here getting into their suspicions anyways. I know these things good considering my memory is the one thing I have going for me, well, that is of course besides the gun. I have my memory and the gun. You can't get much better than that.

People got into their suspicions about me good when me and Mom shacked up in the nice place. Especially that nine-to-fiver Jackson. There's just places some people will never fit in, and it was clear that nobody wanted me or Mom around. Me especially. Most times the only thing that got me out of sticky situations was Dave Treadway. All that guy had to do was open his mouth and everybody listened to every word he said like he was the President of the US of A for chrissakes, or at least the President of good old Fort Harmony, Colorado. All he had to do was say something along the lines of, do you have a problem with my friend, he'd say it just like that, too, and whoever it was that was getting things good and sticky shut the hell up quick.

But I don't have Dave with me today, so I know like there's no tomorrow I'm good and on my own. Besides that fact, I know somebody had to have seen me run out of the bushes like my hair caught fire or something. I wasn't watching my step like I should have been considering Mr. Treadway's a nasty bastard, and he was already in a bad mood that the booze he was drinking would only make worse. I'm no fool so I know there's nothing better I could have done than get the hell out of the bushes fast like I did. But the thing that matters right now is to get the hell out of the park. You have to keep focused sometimes on the things that are happening right at that minute and not what could've happened even one minute ago.

I'm running fast and I don't look around because of my not wanting to know the things that might be going on. Sometimes you have choices like that, to keep your stupid head forward and avoid those things that make you good and crazy. Most times though it's a shame the things you have to have in your head because you didn't have choices not to. Right now I'm glad that I've kept my wits about me and keep looking straight the hell forward. I know there's eyes all around. I keep running extra fast with my hands deep in my coat pockets and my jacket still zipped right to the top. And, like I told you about before, I look funny running like that, but I can't have the gun slipping out of my pocket and ruin my prospects. I have to keep running. I'm hot and my shins hurt bad like they're caught in a gas explosion that caught fire by accident, but I don't stop until I get to the edge of the park and lean up against a nice big tree to try and cool my shins off.

I stand here for a few minutes and try to catch my breath like there's no tomorrow. It's not easy to catch your breath when you're running away from something that turns your stomach inside out like Mr. Treadway does to me. But I finally do catch my breath after a while, and all of a sudden, all I can concentrate on is how hungry I am. And I'm super hungry. It just hits me like a ton of bricks, and just like that, I can't think on anything else. There's a difference between being hungry and just wanting to taste something tasty in your mouth, and being hungry like your stomach is pulling at you from the inside like a giant vacuum cleaner just turned on or something. Like right now, I need food in my stomach like nobody's business.

So just to get my mind off my stomach and my sudden burst of hunger, I start walking again instead of just staying planted against the tree like I'm hoping to grow some leaves my own self. I just walk for a ways because of my not wanting to get out of breath like that again. I don't know how much my lungs can take, and right now, I don't really want to test these kinds of things. You need to keep an eye out for your insides so they don't turn on you and knock you the hell on your ass when you're not looking. Things could get good and ugly if that was the case.

I don't much realize where it is that I've turned to until it's almost too late and I make one big mistake. I'm starting to pass the grocery store again, but I think better of things than to walk right the hell in front of the store again. So I turn down the street just before I get to the grocery store. I don't want to see the lady from the curb again until I can give her something for helping me with Mr. Bones. She didn't do a thing really to help me, but I can't just walk by the grocery store and pretend like I didn't give her my word. Not that it's for sure that she's sitting exactly where she was before, but you can't take your chances on these things.

So I turn down the other street like I told you about before, and walk along the side of the grocery store instead of the front. It's the street with the train tracks that run from one end of town all the way down to the other to wherever the hell it has to go. As I'm passing the side of the grocery store, I hear a whole bunch of people sort of mumble. They're mumbling, but loud so I can hear it. They are saying to praise Jesus. They keep saying it, too, right to my back.

I don't look around because of my knowing I won't see anybody. You just know these things like you know the air you breathe. You can't see it, but it's there just the same. I know it's just the voices. I listen though because of my trying hard to hear that whistle I was telling you about before from Mr. Bones. I put up with the praise Jesus crap just in case I hear that whistle. I don't hear it though and the praise Jesus gets good and on my nerves quick. It's like it's just standing right on my nerves with its heels dug in expecting to stay a good long while. I yell, shut up, loud without much realizing what the hell it is I'm doing and tell them all to go to hell then I start running. I have to get good and far away before the air has swallowed all those useless voices. Now I'm even more hungry and can hardly stand it much less be able to think straight.

I'm walking again, still on the back street and not the busiest street in town either which is a good thing for a lot of reasons that are obvious. I'm no fool you know. Like the last thing I need is to walk by that gypsy lady again. I know like nobody's business she'd get it into her head quick that she needed to get into my business about not being at school like I told her I was going to before. She might give me a weird look because of my hair again and run to the stupid phone and dial for help she doesn't need. Why would I want to do anything to the gypsy lady. She did stop her nice smile when I came out of the bathroom, but you can't try to do anything to try to hurt somebody who helped you out. And the gypsy lady, well, she helped me out good. Deep down though people are just people, and they all get into their suspicions whether they mean to or not. It's just the way of things I guess.

I'm getting far by now, and my head starts working good and takes off all on its own. I don't want it to, but it does it anyways. It's hard to tell your own head to shut the hell up because of most times you don't even realize what it is that it's doing. I figure walking on the tracks is the thing I should do. Like I told you about before, there's trains that ride on these tracks at all times of the day. You need to do things like walk right smack-dab in the middle of train tracks when your head does its own thing and gets the better of you. Prospects ship right the hell into shape when you know like there's no tomorrow that at any minute a train could come along and blow your stupid body right out of your stupid clothes. There's nothing like it to clear your head when you can't shake those no-good voices. I really don't want to think on them anymore. I guess what I really can't shake is Mr. Bones. But like I said before, the tracks can cure all sorts of things when you want something out of your head.

But you can't go fast on the track like you'd like to even if you are wearing white and blue running shoes. You'd think you could go fast because of when you watch the trains they go super-fast and super-cool. I can't go as fast as I need to though, and I can't get the voices to get the hell out of my head. I yell loud and say something along the lines of, Mr. Bones wouldn't piss in the same pot as you much less waste any time talking to you, and then something like, you're all a bunch of crazies stop acting like you know what it is you're talking about. But their voices still won't get the hell out.

So, without much thinking on it, I pull the gun out of my pocket. I wave it around my head like I'm swatting at a dumb fly or something, and I'm yelling loud. I know I am because of my throat starts to itch bad, but I can't hear one little peep. Not one tiny peep like my whole head is under water. I wave the thing around my head and before I know it I'm seeing all black. I feel something wet all over my forehead, and I know like there's no tomorrow I whacked myself good smack-dab in the middle of my forehead.

It should hurt. I know it should hurt considering things like this here always hurt, but I don't feel anything but the wet. Any time there's blood, pain is sure as hell supposed to follow. It's a good thing it happens though considering I have no business waving the thing around in plain view of everybody in the first place. There's eyes everywhere, and I get mad that I lost my head. The pocket is where the thing belongs, not waving around in the air. Stupid. I have the prospects to think on. It's a good thing I can talk myself down or else who knows where the hell I'd be. It's already bad enough that I split my forehead open, but it happened so move on. Always keep moving forward.

CHAPTER EIGHTEEN

Because of my not making the best choices sometimes, I start walking to school. I'm only halfway there by now so I have plenty of other choices than to keep heading to school, but I do it anyhow besides my knowing better. Mom's always good and on my case about my poor choices. She says if there's a wrong choice out there, I'll make it. Who is she to talk anyways. It's not like she's done such a bang-up job moving here from Boston getting a crooked job from that sonofabitch Mike. From where I stand, her choices look less than great. But she's always riding me about it.

Usually I don't agree with the things Mom says, but I know like there's no tomorrow the choice to go to school is a bad one. Laying low like I have been most of the morning is what I need to be doing. But I get to thinking it's not like I have anywhere else to go, and besides that my stomach keeps at me. And when it's your stomach that keeps at you, well, it's all over from there. It's annoying and painful, and you just can't shake the feeling once it's there. What you need is some food, and you can't stop until you get some. I haven't had much of anything in the way of food lately because of it being a slow time for slutty money and a big time for the lottery. Mom has been skimping even more than usual so she can buy out the gas station of all its lottery tickets. She's trying to pass off all sorts of things for a meal. I ate a little of what she fixed last night, but it made me sick. It makes my stomach do somersaults just to think on it now.

So I get to school, and once I'm here, I'm glad. My stomach is screaming by now. Most times when I get to school I don't go in the front doors of the place. Most times I go around to the side door where it's dark and scary where most of my so-called peers wouldn't even step one foot into because of them thinking the echoes in that part of the school are a ghost of somebody they heard about from somebody else who died right in the hallway forever ago. When you live in the bad part of town, things like ghosts don't matter to you much. When you live in the bad part of town, you need to think on things like people like that stupid Brian Farrell and what kind of crappy things your mom is going to try to pass off as dinner. I told you before about how Mom is no chef no matter what she thinks. Ghosts, well, I can take care of ghosts. I know that like there's no tomorrow. All you have to do is put it out of your mind, and then just like that, like the made up stuff ghosts are, it's gone. Poof. Just like that.

Other times when I don't want to bother with anybody at all, I go all the way around to the back of the school. I drag my finger along the brick until I get to the back door that most everybody doesn't even know about because of it being where the janitors get to where it is they need to be. I know where it is considering when you just want to stay the hell away from your peers as much as possible, you know where every door in the place is, and you know exactly who uses it and exactly who doesn't. I know I'm safe from things when I go in the back door. Nobody around here wants to give the janitors the time of day much less go through their door and have to look them in the eyes. People around here don't even want to treat the janitors like they're people. Hell, around here they might as well be one of those ghosts I was telling you about before.

So the choice is easy when I can't even stand one second of getting irritated. I go in the back door and leave the same way. The janitors don't talk to me, and I don't talk to them. They just sit there in the place they're told to go until one of my peers makes a selfish mess that they have to clean up. I don't mess things up for the janitors considering I know how it must be crappy having to clean up after a bunch of no-goods that come around here. I know the way of things with the janitors when it comes to things because of them looking me right in the eyes. I don't need them to say anything. That's all I ask for.

But I'm not going that way today, considering by the time I get to the back door my fingers are usually rubbed raw from the bricks. They get super-red and sting like hell. That would be a bad mistake to do that today considering the prospects I don't want to mess up again. Things could get ugly with raw fingers when you are trying to hold a gun tight in your pocket to keep it the hell out of view of everybody. So I don't go back there today. Today I walk right the hell through the front doors because of my only being here because of the food I'm craving like there's no tomorrow. It's a straight shot to the cafeteria from the front doors.

Lunch has started already. I smell it as soon as I get in the door. The walk took longer than I thought, but at least I made it for lunch. Like I told you about before, I'm a special kind of hungry today like if I don't eat I'm going to lose my stupid mind. What a lucky break that I did decide to come considering it's my favorite lunch today. Waffles and sausages. I don't know how that could've slipped my mind. I always know when it's waffles and sausages day. I can smell it as soon as I get in the doors. If I would've paid attention, my nose could've probably smelled it way the hell back a ways while I was walking up the street, considering your nose can smell all sorts of good when you're extra hungry like I am right at this minute. Waffles and sausages makes for a good lunch, too. Every first Wednesday of the month, it's waffles and sausages. Beautiful.

I walk through the halls fast almost tripping over myself trying to get to the cafeteria as quick as my dumb running shoes will take me. I hate the cafeteria, but I can't think on it now. What I need to think on is getting into the cafeteria and into the line before they close the tall orange doors for business for the day. I almost trip getting through the doors, but I catch myself before I make a mess of things. It would be super embarrassing if I fell and knocked over the cart full of silverware. It's a good thing I caught myself. I hear my stomach extra loud making all kinds of loud noises when I finally get up to the front of the line. It doesn't take too long to get to the front of the line considering just about the whole school is already sitting down and eating by now. But when you're hungry like I am, well, it seems like for-goddamn-ever.

The lunch lady is the same lunch lady who is here everyday. I don't think there's ever been a day when she's not been here. You'd know if your favorite lunch lady wasn't there one day. They aren't all like her. Believe me. She's nice to me when it comes to my lunch. She gives me extra sausages on waffle and sausage day, which makes me even more glad I came today. Somehow she must know that I like to run them through the maple syrup before I eat them or else how would she know to give me extra. It's good that way, with the maple syrup on the sausages. Sure she has lunch lady arms that hang down past her elbow, but that doesn't mean she's not nice. She's friendly like nobody else I know of. She's always giving me free milk, too. Not the milk that sits out on the counter in a bucket of ice that all my so-called peers take their milk from. She pulls mine out of the big silver refrigerator so it's good and extra-cold. Nobody else gets a super-cold milk from that refrigerator.

I think she's so nice to me because of her telling me one time I remind her of her son. She told me he's a downhill skier in the Olympics. I heard all about him because of you don't not listen to somebody tell you a story about their son when they are nice and give you extra-cold milk. I heard all about him. A class-act downhill skier. A real professional that guy. What it is that makes me remind her about her son, I've never figured that one out. I could never be a downhill skier. My legs are too thin, and they'd snap like a measly twig if I ever fell over. They'd twist and tumble all over the place, and just like that, they'd be broken in two. Besides that, my coat would never make it in the cold way up there in the good old Rocky Mountains. It's nice of her to think of me as an upstanding guy though, with me reminding her of her son. Mostly I'm just rough trade, and that's about it. She seems to be the only one around here that thinks otherwise.

Today is no different with the lunch lady. She says a nice hello and looks me right in the eyes. She's loaded me up good today, and I didn't even pay her. I guess she could tell I don't have any money considering she just waved me on past the register. I feel bad, but I didn't have a dime to give to the butterfly lady, and I don't have one to pay for my lunch. But I can't worry on that now. It's best not to look a gift horse in the mouth when it comes to things. At least that's what Mom always says anyhow.

I walk out of the line with my tray. It's full of waffles and sausages and cold milk. I'm so hungry I can't wait to sit down. I'm so hungry I forget my manners and don't say thank you to the lunch lady. I feel like hell for not saying thank you, but I'm that special kind of hungry and can't wait to sit down. None of my so-called peers ever say thank you to the lunch lady. It's kind of like the same thing with the janitors around this place. Hell, they don't even take the time to look up from wherever the hell it is that they're looking that is so important to say hello. But they always take the time to irritate her because of her having to wear one of those net things on her head. It gets me mad when they do that considering she wears it because of she probably knows that nobody wants somebody else's hair in their food. She's just being considerate to people who are crappy on the inside. Where's the justice in that. Today I wouldn't mind one little bit if there was a hair in my waffles and sausages because of when you're real hungry like I am right now, your stomach just says to hell with it. You eat whatever it is that can make its way into your starving mouth.

Besides the fact that I'm hungry and want to sit down quick so I can eat, it's hard to hold the tray with just my left hand. I can't hold it with both hands for reasons that we all know about, with my right hand stuck in my coat pocket. Not that I'm weak or anything with having to hold the tray with one hand. I'm walking cool and tough, but I don't feel like it's going so well. It's just good and awkward to carry a lunch tray with just your left hand, especially when you're used to doing everything under the sun with your right hand. It's tough to balance something like a lunch tray with just one hand. I feel like my wrist might crack right in two if I'm not careful and find a seat where I can put my tray down quick.

I see only one empty table. It's right in the middle of the cafeteria for chrissakes. Most times I get to the cafeteria first so I pick wherever the hell it is I want to sit. But today I'm late considering my morning. Most times I'm early enough to pick a table where I can sit with my back to the wall. Nobody can flick things at your head when you sit with your back to the wall. Nobody will flick anything to the front of your head so you can see who the hell it is and so you can say something tough-like to them. They only flick things to the back of your head considering most times people don't want to take responsibilities for doing something as crappy as that. I figured that one out a long time ago. Probably my very first day with my peers in this place, so it's been me sitting with my back to the wall ever since. It's the only way I can eat in some peace around here. Everybody should get to eat in some peace and quiet. That's the way things should be anyways.

I look down at my food that has slipped to the edge of my tray and almost fallen off because of my wrist getting tired. I can't let anything happen to my food. There's nothing I can do except walk to the only empty table in the whole cafeteria. So with me having no other choice in the matter, I sit down in the seat where there's a spotlight just sort of shining down right where I have to sit. It only happens because of there being a light out right next to the one that's on, but it's enough to make you feel like it's a spotlight and you're right on stage. So I take a seat and the first thing I notice is how the buzz from the lights is annoying and louder from here than where I usually sit with my back against the wall. I notice it right off the bat. My stomach doesn't seem to mind though. It just wants those waffles and sausages like there's no tomorrow.

I sit down and plan to dig in right away. I plan on eating fast considering how my stomach is nagging me and how I want to be anywhere but here that's good and out of the spotlight. Anyways, I sit down and open up the milk carton and cut up my sausages with the edge of my fork right away like I like them. I do it with my left hand and keep the right one in my coat pocket. I don't take off my shoes like usual considering how much of a hurry I'm in. Usually that's first on the list, but today, there's just no time for those kinds of things today. I don't take my coat off either, but then again, I never take my coat off for lunch. I keep it zipped right to the top.

CHAPTER NINETEEN

It's awkward to eat today because of my having to eat with my left hand. I don't take my right hand out of my coat pocket with the gun needing to be held and protected. I learned my lesson at the college. It would be dumb of me to ruin the prospects before I think through them again. Things could get ugly, and I'm no fool. So I concentrate on holding the gun tight but smooth in my pocket. I'm running the cut up pieces of sausage around in the maple syrup like I was telling you before how I like to do. My mouth can hardly stand the teasing though, and I feel like if I open it one little crack a gush of water will come running out. I guess I can handle the torment considering I know what a treat I'm in for if I can hold off long enough to get the pieces of sausage good and covered in the maple syrup.

My mouth is good and ready to go. My lips are practically quivering waiting to get the first bite the hell on my tongue. But then, all of a sudden, before I can even take my first bite of lunch, I hear somebody cawing behind me. I have the fork almost in my mouth when it happens. I can taste it even before it hits my mouth. I feel a dribble of that hungry water fall off my lower lip right in the middle. I know who it is that's cawing at me without even having to turn around because it's the same ugly deep voice I hear every other day. It's that stupid Brian Farrell.

Brian Farrell is one of those dainty guys who are into things like their hair and how fast they can pop a muscle through their shirt. He gets all the girls to do and say whatever the hell he wants because of them going weak in the knees if he just looks at them sideways or something. Me, well, that's a whole different thing. I have a nice face and pretty teeth, too, just like Mom, but everybody's too hung up on my being rough trade and too busy cawing to notice. It's just as well though, considering naked makes me sick. But not good old Brian Farrell. He'll run around school with his shirt off just like there's no tomorrow. It's those squatty little muscles that he's super into showing off. Nobody ever asks him to do a thing like take off his shirt. He just does it and gets one hell of a kick out of it. He's good and into being naked.

Who the hell wants somebody heckling them right to the back of their head when all they do is sit there and try to eat their lunch in some peace. What I can't figure on is how anybody even noticed me in the first place. I don't do anything to draw attention to myself ever. I can't recall ever saying one word to my so-called peers, not one little peep really, and all they can think on is to irritate me. Irritating people sure does seem to take a lot out of your day, but my so-called peers will caw till the cows come home just to make me feel good and rotten. Somebody always has to feel good and rotten. It's just the way of things around here.

Like I know that stupid Brian Farrell has plenty of other things to think on besides me. About as many as there are hours in the day if I count things correctly. Who knows, maybe the more things you have to account for and worry on everyday of your life, the more things you think you have to think on and worry about. Like take me. I know I'm going to have to wake up tomorrow and the day after that and the day after that and sometimes just knowing that all on its own is enough to keep my head going for a long time. But not that Brian Farrell. He has to worry about things every single second of the day and just uses me as the filler between deciding on what color of socks he should wear to go with his dainty sweater and worrying about Mr. Robbins not giving him an A just because of him shining his pearly whites and flexing his hairy peckerwood.

Is it too much to ask to eat lunch in some peace without being irritated for chrissakes. Is it too much to ask that just one day, just one measly day could go like I have it in my head. You know the kind of day where people have some manners and say hello to you when they should and keep their stupid mouth shut when you're trying to eat your waffles and sausages. For chrissakes, doesn't that guy know it's waffles and fucking sausages day. It's not a good day to caw at me or irritate me. Not a good goddamn day. What the hell gets in these peoples heads around here. Don't they know today it would be best just to leave me the fuck alone.

I try hard to just let it roll off my back like you're supposed to do in these situations, and I do good until I hear my other peers join in. Cawing. I know deep down from the start that they're going to join in considering they always join in when it comes to Brian Farrell, but I still get mad. You can always tell it in the air when Brian Farrell starts in on his crap how it's going to be like a goddamn avalanche or something. He's like that shot from some dumb bastard at the bottom of a mountain that gets the snow rolling smothering every damn thing that gets in its way. It always starts with him opening his big fat mouth to caw like he's so clever, and before you know it, it's things being flicked to the back of your head like a chewed-up piece of gum that gets good and stuck in your hair, and you can only get it out by going home and using a kitchen knife to shave it the hell out.

I get hot now, and I want to take my coat off bad, but I don't. I keep it zipped to the top. Sometimes if I just ignore whatever the hell it is they're saying, they'll shut up, so I try it. It seems to calm down for a minute. Then somebody says something about my haircut. Some girl. Some worthless girl feels the need to say something about my haircut. It's my haircut for chrissakes, it's none of her business, right. My business is my business. I was hot you motherfucking girl. HOT.

It gets me mad thinking how regular people that have it good don't know they have it good. They don't know anything about being rough trade. I know how their heads work because of my seeing it first hand when we lived right smack-dab in the middle of all sorts of regular people. There's just things you know about regular people that makes them super-comfortable with themselves so they can caw at other people and irritate them like crazy. Like my stupid peers with them having regular parents. Who doesn't want a real mom. Hell, who doesn't want a real dad, for that matter. Not some smartie that wears all that damn corduroy and can't recognize his son that looks just like the floozy from the shop he threw one into. I look just like her. God, I hate corduroy.

Most times they don't know their luck, but I know their luck. It's enough to get good and under your skin sometimes with them not appreciating it. You know, with them making fun of a guy's haircut for chrissakes. Sometimes I just want to yell at them and say something important like, you just don't know how good you have it, but I don't because of my knowing the way they would look at me like I'm stupid for saying things like that. But it still gets me that they irritate me like they do. I'd know if I had it good. I'd enjoy the hell out of it. And right now, well, right now is the closest I've come with my having the prospects on my side in my right coat pocket. I would never irritate a guy because of a haircut.

Somehow I know the voice, you know the stupid girl's voice who felt the need to say something about my haircut. It sounds familiar and before I know it, I know like there's no tomorrow, like a water balloon busted all over my shoulder or something, that it's Candy Carmichael's voice. Let me tell you something, I'm seeing red by now. I think I'm hearing wrong because of Candy Carmichael being nice and OK in my book, but I memorized that voice a long time ago. She sounds different from the other girls around this place. The other girls around here, well, their voices are squeaky and can drive you up a wall most times. It gets me mad right now just thinking on it, and it makes me shiver thinking how it just grates right the hell up your spine.

But Candy Carmichael has a voice like a piano. She sounds just like somebody is playing a song of beauty right on a piano. Who doesn't want to listen to a song of beauty out of a pretty thing like a piano. When she raises her hand in Mr. Robbins's class to answer a question, I close my eyes and listen good. With my eyes closed, it feels like it's just me she's talking to. Sometimes I can't handle how it makes me feel inside, like my heart forgot how to beat the right way or something. Closing your eyes to listen to such a thing of beauty like that, well, it'll blow you out of your stupid head. Right now though I'd rather be hearing anything but that. It makes me feel bad like I've never felt bad before to hear that Candy Carmichael's voice now. That stupid Brian Farrell can ruin anything for chrissakes. Even a voice like a piano.

I'm seeing everything red by now. It's all over. There is red in every stupid thing. Even the extra-cold milk the lunch lady gave me for free is red. I squint hard, but it doesn't help. The red just stays, and it's good and hard to stay cool when you start seeing red. So just like my hair caught fire or something, I stand up quick without not much knowing what I'm doing. My head is foggy, and I can hardly steady myself but I turn around cool. I turn around slow, and they all start laughing like something is funny. It echoes good in my ears.

I can see Candy Carmichael sitting right next to that stupid Brian Farrell. She's not laughing. She's just looking down at her lunch roll and won't look up. So I'm standing here and everybody but Candy Carmichael is still laughing at me. I just want them to stop. I just want Candy Carmichael to look up and say something in her piano voice so I can close my eyes and listen and fall away from where it is I am right at this minute. She doesn't look up though. No matter how hard I stare, she doesn't look up. I'm wore out and hungry, and all I want is to close my eyes and listen to Candy Carmichael and eat my waffles and sausages.

The people behind me are even laughing by now. I look around to see the laughing. For once, I want to see who it is that's doing all the laughing. It's all one big blur of open mouths, laughing loud and laughing hard all around me. My head starts to sweat. I know my face is red. I hold the gun tight, and pull it out of my coat pocket smooth. I hold it just right, just like I practiced, so I know I look tough. I'm angry, but I do good at holding the gun right into all the laughing. Suddenly something's not so goddamn funny. They all shut the hell up like I wanted, but the echo of them laughing won't go the hell away.

Even with the echoes, I know that suddenly they have to look at me and know I'm done fucking around. I just hold it there for a while and keep the silence in the room uncomfortable. I keep it tense because of the prospects coming to life. I need to shake my bad feeling from deep inside. Candy Carmichael is just like all the rest. Just another worthless girl. I'm saying right to myself, you always need to keep your wits about you, Dusty, even if her voice is a thing of beauty. Never, never let a girl into your head like that. Keep your eye on the prize, my friend. Eye on the prize. You need to appreciate things when they happen. People need to appreciate good things that happen to them when they happen. It might make for a little more happiness around this place.

So I'm blinking hard, and I'm sweaty by now and just like that I hear somebody say hello to me. It sounds far away, but I can hear it clear. Can't they tell I'm right in the middle of something important. Hell, I'm right in the middle of something, and somebody thinks that now is a good time to say hello. He says, hello Dusty. He uses my name just like that to make sure I know he's talking to me. I look to my right where the noise is coming from, and who do I see but Mr. Robbins. I can't see his face considering it's blurry, but I know it's him because of his sweater.

He's always wearing this green button-down sweater. Even when it gets hot outside, he's always wearing that green sweater. It's a good color, it's not that. Who doesn't like green anyways. Don't get me wrong, I like the sweater considering Mr. Robbins is a stand-up guy. Anything he does is pretty much OK with me. It's just that he's always wearing the same green sweater.

He keeps walking towards me. I start to see his face because of it not being so blurry when he gets closer to me. That guy though, Mr. Robbins, just needs to learn when to stick his nose in your business and when not to. Your business is your business, and right now this is my business. My back is sweaty, and I'm still super-hot. He says to me, you don't look so good, and asks if I'm OK. He doesn't even mention the gun, and it's right in my stupid hand. Right in plain view of everybody.

It's like Mr. Robbins is trying to have one of those heart-to-hearts he always likes to have. I don't ever see him trying to have a whole lot of heart-to-hearts with all my other peers around this place. Maybe he knows my so-called peers are a waste like I know they're a waste. But he always seems to pick the wrong time to ask me the way things are going. Most times he grabs me on the way out of his classroom and makes me extra-late to wherever it is I'm going to get to next so he can ask the way of things in my life. Most times, I'm just wanting to follow Candy Carmichael and her good smell some more, and that's what he's getting in the way of. It's like he's doing that right now, but how do you tell somebody like Mr. Robbins that now's not a good time for a heart-to-heart.

I tell him not to take one more goddamn step at me, and he stays right the hell where I told him to because of that being what I wanted. I don't want Mr. Robbins to be involved in this. I wish like there's no tomorrow that he would be where all the other teachers in this place go to eat their lunch. In the stupid teachers lounge, where I know they sit around and talk to each other about things like how good Candy Carmichael smells. Candy Carmichael. What a thing for her to do. I squeeze my eyes together to keep from blowing my worthless top at that one. Candy Carmichael. But I can't think on that now. Just stop it. Stop it. Stop.

OK.

There's just things in this world you can't do, and you can't lose your cool in times like these here. I know like nobody's business that what I'm saying is the truth. So I open my eyes again, and I see Mr. Robbins still standing right the hell where I told him to. But he's bending over and picking something up from a filthy cafeteria table. I say to him, what the hell are you doing Mr. Robbins. He stands up again slow with some white things in his hand. I say, what the hell is that Mr. Robbins. He says, it's napkins.

I say, why the hell are you picking up napkins when you know I could blow your head clean off your body if I wanted to. He says, I know Dusty but your forehead is bleeding and I was going to give you napkins to clean it up.

At first, I'm not believing what Mr. Robbins is telling me, but then I start to feel the blood thick and creeping out of my head. My forehead gets wet again like it was when it first happened that I split my head open. It's wet and sticky. I put it out of my mind though because of times like this one here only come along once or twice in your lifetime. And, well, me, I'm lucky that it came along for me at all considering I'm rough trade and these once or twice in a lifetime occasions don't come into our lives too often. Sometimes not even the once or twice that they're supposed to. You can't worry about things that might come up and take away your momentous occasion like it was never supposed to happen. I'm making it happen and good, too, if I may say so myself.

But like I was telling you about before, I wish like there's no tomorrow that Mr. Robbins would have been with the rest of the stupid teachers around this place, far away from this situation here. But he's right there in front of me holding napkins, being the stand-up guy that he is even when he thinks I could blow his head to pieces. I tell him I don't need any of his napkins and can't he see that I'm right in the middle of something for chrissakes. He says he's sorry and puts the napkins back down. Goddamnit. Why does he have to be like that. Things could get ugly fast, and the things he's doing are good and nice. I feel the blood that's coming from my forehead roll down the side of my nose and another bead that leaks down and gets caught right in my eyebrow. Right in my albino-like eyebrow that I know like nobody's business that it will stain. It's super-hard to get blood out of your albino eyebrows. It'll take days. But I can't think on that now. The prospects are still alive and well.

Before I know it, he's right next to me and puts his hand on my shoulder. I know he's doing it in a nice way, you know in a Mr. Robbins sort of a way, but I don't like it. Who likes another guy putting his hands on your shoulder when you're trying to look tough with a gun in your hand. I don't. So I fart. I blow a big one, and I know the smell will be bad because of my eating some of what Mom fixed for dinner last night. My stomach has been a wreck ever since. It tasted like hell. Nobody, I don't care who you are, likes the smell of somebody else's fart. I know it smells bad and nasty. You know the kind that makes it good and hard to breathe.

It works just as good as I thought. Mr. Robbins takes a few steps back. Nobody likes the smell of somebody else's fart. I look at him, not in the face but in the chest right at that green sweater, and I tell him this doesn't concern him. It's not his business. It's just that somebody's always getting taken and most times that somebody is me. But not today. I'm not getting taken today. He takes it good and stays where he is. I don't even point the gun at him, and he doesn't ignore me. What a stand-up guy that Mr. Robbins.

But as all good things do, the smell fades, and it's not so hard to get close to me. Don't get me wrong, it takes a while for it to vanish into thin air like those people that claim they were abducted by aliens in the middle of a corn field, but it goes away quicker than I would like. Most times it stays long enough to get whatever the hell it is I need to get done done but not today. There's just too much riding on today. Now I know things would have been better off if I'd have just kept it cool with that stupid Brian Farrell and the rest of my peers. I'm running out of things quick. I'm hot and my eyes sting good. Maybe Mom knows better of things by sleeping right in the middle of the day and not having to deal with crap. I might not get so irritated by things if I took a lesson or two from Mom.

I'm pointing the gun still and steady right at my so-called peers, and all of a sudden, all I can see is Mr. Robbins's red face right in front of my eyes. He stayed away for a while because of that ass I blew, but now he's standing right in front of me. His nose is almost touching me for chrissakes. He's saying a bunch of stuff that I know he thinks is important in that what-I'm-saying-is-important voice, but I don't hear a word of it. How I know he's talking is by my being able to see his mouth moving. It's all blurry and all I see is white and red moving around, but it's hard to ignore a mouth moving when it's right in front of your stupid face. I wonder how he got that close, but there's no time to wonder on those things.

I'm sliding fast, and I can't do a goddamn thing about it now because of Mr. Robbins being a heroic kind of a guy and taking the gun right out of my hand. My head's a wreck, and I get dizzy. All I want is my gun back. My head is going fast around and around, and just like that, I puke on Mr. Robbins. The last thing I want to do is puke yellow gut juice all over Mr. Robbins's favorite green button-down sweater that he wears every stupid day. It smells like hell, too. Most times when I feel like I'm going to puke, I don't considering nobody likes to puke so I avoid it by thinking on other things like punching Mike the sonofabitch right square in his crooked teeth. But today, well, there's just too much going on today to concentrate like I'd need to to keep it the hell in.

So right away after I puke on Mr. Robbins, I want to apologize like nobody's business, but things get interrupted because of some stupid girl way in the back of the cafeteria starting to cry like a little baby. It's always the girls ruining good things in my life. Suddenly, since I don't have the prospects anymore, all this noise fills my head. More stupid girls start their crying like they caught a cold from the first girl for chrissakes. It makes me sick to my stomach again to think of girls crying just because another girl started it. I puke again all over the floor this time, which is better than on Mr. Robbins. It hits the floor with a splat like I just turned a bucket of water over and it hit the floor quick. When you don't have anything in your stomach other than gut juice, that's what happens.

I look at that stupid Brian Farrell and the look on his face for just one second. I wish I had a snapshot of the look on his face. His mouth is open wide, and he's super-pale. It's hard for somebody that has a tan all year to get that pale, but I'm seeing it right before my very eyes. He's just sitting there like he's holding his pecker in his hand. He doesn't seem so cool now, does he. Caw now you little prick. Laugh into my face now. I dare you. I only get to look for a second though considering Mr. Robbins wants to get me the hell out of the cafeteria. I still want to apologize for what I did to his sweater, but Mr. Robbins is in too much of a hurry for those things.

With all those stupid girls and their crying, it's not such a bad thing to have to leave the cafeteria. It gets under my skin good and quick. I told you before about how their voices are squeaky and can drive you up a wall, and when they start in on their crying, it's even worse. Mr. Robbins has me by the elbow and walks me back the same way it was that I came to sit down at this filthy place, right in the middle of the cafeteria. There's no other way to do it I guess. It's just right down the middle of the cafeteria right in front of God and everybody. And like I told you before, I can't figure on which is worse.

For some reason, I look up from where I'm looking at the floor, and I see the lunch lady peeking her head out of the tall orange lunch line doors. Mr. Robbins is trying to get me the hell out of Dodge, but I look right into her face and she's looking right into mine. I wish like hell she would have just stayed back in the lunch line room, back by the big silver refrigerator and kept paying attention to the tasty food she serves. She doesn't need to worry herself with the kinds of things that are going on here. So I'm looking right into her face and I remember that I forgot my manners and never said a nice thank you for the extra sausages I never got to eat. She deserves a nice thank you because of what she did. Giving me the extra sausages was a nice thing to do.

She's looking at me sad, and I wish like there's no tomorrow things like this situation here, with somebody like Mr. Robbins dragging you away from your prospects, would stay far away from nice people like the lunch lady. I think quick on how I can make that sad look on her face go away. I want to tell her maybe I'll take up skiing just to make her happy and forget about my losing my manners. Not that I could ever get up to the Rocky Mountains or anything, but I would say it just to make her happy. But before I can get out one little peep to make up for my losing my manners,

Mr. Robbins gives one good yank on my arm to keep my feet moving the hell forward. Like I told you about before, Mr. Robbins is just in too big a hurry for me to make a sincere apology to anybody.

CHAPTER TWENTY

So now I have to go to the office, and I don't get to eat my lunch which irritates things. When am I going to eat. I'm super-hungry, and I don't get to eat because of that stupid Brian Farrell and the prospects getting the better of me. Why can't he mind his own business for once. My business is my business, right. All I wanted was to eat my waffles and sausages in some peace and quiet. And that Candy Carmichael. She doesn't even know what the hell she's talking about with bad haircuts or bad names for that matter. Where did she get it in her head that she needs to irritate me, too. She was pretty OK in my book. I know it's that stupid Brian Farrell. That guy gets on my nerves good. But that doesn't matter much considering how Mr. Robbins is walking me down the hall to the office like I'm a stupid kid for chrissakes. Like I can't walk by myself or something. I'm not a kid though. Right now I'm just hungry and want those waffles and sausages like nobody's business.

My stomach seems to be last on the list though. I'm stuck with Mr. Robbins walking me down the hall like I'm a stupid kid or something else that can't take care of itself. He keeps saying how the stupid school psychologist is going to fix my head. Let me tell you something, there's nothing wrong with my head. My head is clear as a bell right now. I know the way of things better than anybody. What is wrong right now though is that Mr. Robbins is carrying my gun and not me. That's what's wrong right now. He's carrying the thing by the barrel, and doesn't know how to hold it just right to make it look tough or at least a little intimidating. I know exactly how to carry the thing. I'd show him a thing or two if he'd just give it back to me because of Mr. Robbins being a stand-up guy. He deserves to know the prospects and how to hold the gun the right way to make him look tough. He needs to hold it just right.

What a time to have to go to the office. During my lunchtime. Right in the middle of waffles-and-goddamn-sausage day. That's what really gets to me. During my lunch that I haven't gotten one little goddamn bite of. Who the hell has to go to see the principal or the stupid school psychologist during lunch for chrissakes. Don't they know I have to eat. Couldn't things wait until after I ate my lunch. I don't ask for a whole lot from this lousy place. Mr. Robbins keeps mumbling to himself barely loud enough for me to hear about how I should hope hard on them not expelling me from school considering those crappy plastic water guns aren't even allowed on school property much less any kind of thing like I had here. Like that would be such a bad thing, being expelled from school. Mom would sure as hell be mad if I got expelled though. She just likes me good and out of her hair. Forget about her though. Taking away my waffles and sausages, well, that's really what's bad here.

When does he think I'm supposed to eat. There's no perfect little Mrs. Robbins at my house to cook. It's just Mom who's no chef no matter what she thinks. The crap she makes, except for the TV dinners, well, nobody wants to eat the crap she makes when she decides to make it. I just don't get why I can't eat my waffles and sausages. The thing doesn't even work. It's not like I could've done anything. It's not like I could pull the trigger and take off that stupid Brian Farrell's face like I wanted to. It's too late now though to just go back and pretend things are normal. Somebody probably already threw away all the extra sausages the lunch lady was nice enough to give me. Where the hell do these people learn to live anyways.

So I guess I'm not walking down the stupid hall as fast as Mr. Robbins thinks I should be. I can tell this because of him wrapping his long fingers around the top of my arm tight. Because of him being so tall, his hands are extra-big and almost fit around my whole arm for chrissakes. He's taller than I am. There aren't a whole lot of people around this place that are, so his hand gets good and right up there. And I know like there's no tomorrow it's good and swampy up there in my armpit. There are just some things you can tell, and right now, I can tell I'm good and swampy like nobody's business. You have to hand it to Mr. Robbins for just not dropping his hand quick after touching my sweaty armpit. Nobody I know would keep a tight hold on somebody else's sweaty parts.

But, I guess based on how tight Mr. Robbins keeps hold of my arm, I can know he wants me to get the hell into the office and off his hands quick. He holds me tight like I'm a slimy fish or something, and a slimy fish he doesn't want to get away. It's not like I could anyways. But he can hold a guy tight, that's for sure. There's just things you can tell, and right now, I can tell by the way he's holding my arm tight that he wants me in the office and out of his hair. The faster the better. I figure that's why he makes me walk fast. I'm almost tripping over myself to keep up for crying out loud.

Then he says it out loud and lets me know I'm right about the suspicions I got into. He says it out loud, right in front of me, about him not being equipped to deal with this shit. He keeps saying it just like that, not equipped to deal with this shit. I lose my balance because of my never hearing Mr. Robbins throw the cuss bomb like that before with him being such a stand-up guy. Let me tell you something, I sure didn't figure on a stand-up guy like Mr. Robbins throwing the cuss bomb around like that. Talk about being thrown for one hell of a loop.

He keeps talking to himself like he's carrying on a whole conversation with two people. But there's really not two people he's talking to. I know like nobody's business that it's not me he's talking to, so there must be somebody in his head that's answering right back. It happens to me a lot, too, and I know it's just best not to interrupt those kinds of things. The world will see all kinds of ugly when you interrupt somebody when they're having a conversation going on in their own head. It's a whole world you don't want to blow up just by saying something and shorting a fuse or something.

I hear a bunch of rustling going on behind me. It gets even louder than Mr. Robbins and his grumbling. Without even having eyes in the back of my head, I know like there's no tomorrow that some of my stupid peers followed us out of the cafeteria and down this hallway just to irritate things. Like things aren't already irritated enough. There's footsteps that are soft, but not soft enough that I can't hear that they're there. I can also hear their whispering to the person next to them. You can't tell when it's a guy or a stupid girl when they're whispering like they are.

My head starts playing tricks on me and doing things all on its own. All I start hearing is to praise Jesus. At first it's soft, but then it gets louder. Goddamnit. That's the last thing I need on my plate right at this minute, so all you praise Jesus freaks get the hell out. I almost lose my marbles again because of Mr. Bones walking across my mind. They knew they'd get good and in my head if they talked on Mr. Bones and how I needed to pray to Jesus for him. He's walking right across my mind. Walking on his knees with his bones crunching together like a mouthful of teeth chomping on nothing but the air it gets for free. Please no more. I can't stand it. Please.

STOP.

I guess I'm talking out loud because of all of a sudden everything is quiet and stopped just like I said. There's no footsteps and no whispering and no Mr. Robbins carrying on conversations with himself. He's looking at me in the face, but I don't look at him in the eyes. I look down at his hand holding my gun. I want to grab it, turn around, and hold it in all the faces and the whispers I know are going to come back any minute now from my peers. But I can't think on it too much though because of Mr. Robbins reading my thoughts like they're written right the hell across my forehead or something. And just like that, I don't see his hand anymore because of he gets smart and holds it behind his back. Almost in the same minute as that, I find my feet moving again and me being pushed forward.

We've made it through the hallway in no-time flat and are in the office. Whoever thought up offices anyways. Like this one in particular. It feels like hell in here. The heat is going full blast for chrissakes. Don't they know it's hot outside all on its own. I'm hot as hell myself. I might lose myself if I think too much more on it. Mr. Robbins lets go of my arm as soon as we're in the office and closes the door tight behind him. I know how things work most times, and I'd bet money as soon as Mr. Robbins gets to get the hell out of here, like I know he'd like to like nobody's business, he's going to beeline it for the bathroom and wash his hands good and raw. Nobody, I don't care who you are, likes the smell of somebody else on their hands for any longer than it has to be there. Things are good and ripe down there right now. He's going to have to wash for a while to get the smell good and gone.

I'm not even going to mention the green sweater that I yakked on accidentally. I know that thing is probably going to make its way into the trash before he gets home to his nice little Mrs. Robbins so she doesn't have to know that there's things in this world that are good and rotten. He tells me to sit down and points to a chair in the corner. It looks uncomfortable and hard, but I do it anyhow because of my not wanting to hear Mr. Robbins cuss again. I know it's right on the tip of his tongue. I'm no fool about these things you know. You can just tell when somebody who is mad about something and super-irritable just has cuss words all over the place inside their mouth. But Mr. Robbins, well, there's somebody you don't want to hear that from. He's not like Mike the sonofabitch when it comes to that.

CHAPTER TWENTY-ONE

It's about time my so-called peers came face to face with a bad situation. Turning tables like I did today keeps everybody right the hell on their toes. It's a thing of beauty to do that every once in a while. I'd be a lot more optimistic though if I hadn't landed myself where I am right this minute. The office isn't the place you want to be if you're dragged here, away from your moment, your one time to shine, away from the cafeteria all because of you finally had the balls to say enough is enough. This is the last place you want to be. You want to still be having your moment.

I know why it's a big deal, about the gun. You'd have to be a fool not to know the potentials in a situation like having a gun in the school cafeteria. I'm headed straight for the books with this one. I know exactly why it is that it's a big deal. Especially for somebody like Mr. Robbins who had to see the whole ugly truth from beginning to end. I've never seen the guy turn so many different colors of red before, and to be honest, I never want to see it again. You can just tell that things for Mr. Robbins have always been smooth sailing. Nothing has ever gotten into his life and did anything good and rotten, so this situation here, it's a big one. I hate that I was the one who did a number on Mr. Robbins and the way he's used to things. But besides that I hate that he was the one who dragged me here from the cafeteria. I thought we had a thing going, Mr. Robbins and me.

He should have just been with the rest of the teachers in this place eating his lunch in some peace in the teachers lounge. Not the cafeteria for chrissakes. What kind of a teacher goes to the cafeteria for lunch. I'm not saying it's not a big deal, I wanted it to be a big deal, but if Mr. Robbins took half a stupid second after he interrupted things, he'd know the worthless thing is no good anyhow. It wouldn't do one little thing even if my hand got the better of things and gave a little pull. But Mr. Robbins didn't take the half a second, so I'm sitting here on this hard-ass chair instead of hopping down the bunny trail like I would be if things had gone my way.

Who wants to sit here in a chair that's made for somebody half your size that Mr. Robbins put you in for the sole purpose of thinking what you did was bad especially when you can't think it's bad your own self. You've never seen a whole bunch of people shut the hell up quick until you have a gun in your hand. It's a thing of beauty. Most times things that happen are hard enough to stomach the first time around, but today, I want to memorize all the things about today. I wish I could pin the look on every single one of their faces on my wall. Hell, I might even tape the look on their faces up in my locker. Those are some pictures I'd put up there. Beautiful.

But I start to feel bad for Mr. Robbins who just can't seem to catch his breath. He's standing by the counter, bracing himself with his right arm, and holding my gun clumsy in his left hand. He's breathing hard and quick. I'm afraid he might take a header if he doesn't calm down soon. Sucking in that much air all at once isn't good for anybody. I don't want anything to happen to Mr. Robbins. I try to tell him that the thing is no good and that I couldn't hurt anybody no matter how much I wanted to. I try hard to get his attention to say what I have to say, but I can tell by the look that he shoots me with his red eyes that he just wants me to sit here and that's it.

It's hot in here, and I wish like hell they would turn down the heater. Better yet, turn the dumb thing off. My coat is starting to rub on my neck right up under my chin, and I can't hardly stand it. My neck and hands get swelled up when I'm hot and I can't move around. When I'm like this, I need to move the hell around so my blood keeps moving where it's supposed to go. But, of course, I'm stuck in this stupid chair. It doesn't happen very often that my coat rubs like it is, but when it does, it's about enough to make you go out of your head. I know it's that stupid office lady on the other side of the counter who keeps the heater racked up to about 80 degrees. She must think she's on a tropical island or something wearing a sun dress like she is. I don't know why she even bothered with a dress anyways. It's not covering much of anything a dress should cover. Who does she think she is for chrissakes.

It's hard to think when you're so hot you can hardly stand it. And besides that, it's even harder to think on anything else when all you can concentrate on is the office lady in her low-cut sun dress and cheap press-on fingernails. Naked makes me sick, and so do those nails. I know they're the cheap press-on kind because of my seeing Mom put them on every time she has one of her dates. They are always pink. What the hell is her deal with pink anyways. She's always getting stuck on one thing or the other, and the nails, well, the nails are the least of my worries when it comes to Mom.

The office lady is acting just the way Mom does when she has on those cheap press-on nails. Mr. Robbins is trying like hell to talk to her, but she's just going to take her sweet time to give him what he wants. I know she hears him. How can you not hear somebody who is standing almost right in your face saying things like, excuse me Miss Office Lady. I know she can hear him, but other things are just more important to her right now like talking to some other office lady with a big fat ass who's laughing at something the first office lady is saying like she has a goldfish stuck in her throat or something.

What do they think is going on here for chrissakes. Those office ladies need to ship the hell into shape. It's not everyday Mr. Robbins runs in the office like his hair caught fire. But it's hard to get somebody's attention who wears those crappy press-on nails. I know this for a fact. Mr. Robbins has a lot of talking ahead of him. They just want people to look at them and say things like, do you want to go out sometime, or, you smell like a real gem today. But he's not saying those things. He's saying things like, we have a real serious situation here Miss Office Lady. Real serious. That's what he said, just like that. Now I know it's the prospects that count considering the words real serious have never been used in the same sentence with my name before. You know things mean something when somebody says something like real serious.

Mr. Robbins finally gets fed up and gets smart about the whole thing and holds my gun right in the office lady's face. He does it good and I don't even have to tell him the way of things on how to hold it just right. He says the same thing again about having a real serious situation. It took him a while, but he finally caught on to what it was he had to do to get somebody like that's attention. When I see how she perks her little tits and ears right up when she sees my gun, well, it's a thing of beauty. Mr. Robbins should realize it's my gun and my prospects. He should give it back and let me go on my merry way for chrissakes.

The lady with the big fat ass just disappeared. I didn't even see where the hell it is she went to. It's hard to hide a big fat ass like that, so she must've been good and scared, and shot out of here quick like a big fat fire was lit right under her big fat ass. The office lady though, she can't go anywhere because of her having to stand right where she is behind the counter and do her dumb job.

Real serious. I'm going to remember that and write it on my tombstone. Beautiful. I'm not one of those people who will have R.I.P. on their tombstone. Rest In Peace. How the hell else do you rest except in peace for chrissakes. I don't get a whole lot of peace when I try to sleep at night, but it's a whole different thing when you're dead and when you're just trying to get a little shut-eye. None of that R.I.P. crap for me. It's going to say Real Serious. Better make it all caps, REAL SERIOUS. Beautiful.

So now the office lady seems to have all kinds of things to say to Mr. Robbins. And he somehow found that breath he was losing quick before when the office lady finally decided to give her attention to him and the situation at hand instead of concentrating on her own crappy self. Nobody's talking to me still, which is fine by me right at the moment. Who wants to talk to somebody when all their prospects just got ruined by the do-gooder Mr. Robbins. Things about Mr. Robbins are sure going downhill fast in my head.

I don't let it bug me that Mr. Robbins and the office lady are talking about me right in front of my face. I hear them talking about me like I'm not even here. Like I'm not point-blank right here for chrissakes. She asks all nosy, what went wrong, and Mr. Robbins starts telling her things that don't add up for me. He's telling her things that are going on in my head. Nobody knows what goes on in my head though. He's not telling her how I looked tough and had control of the whole entire place, he's talking about my stupid head. Then, just like a field caught fire and spread through the whole damn thing or something, they both start to have their opinions as to my state of mind on why I'm sitting here in this chair that is a pain in my ass. That's what they call it, too, my state of mind. They get so high on their stupid horse like they're Einstein or somebody else who is smart and figuring me out like a useless science project or something. But I'm not a stupid science project, and they aren't Einstein like they like to think they are.

I see Mr. Robbins lean in close to the office lady. I know he's saying something else quiet so I can't hear, not that I want to anyways, and all of a sudden, the office lady looks up at me with pity. Her head tilts to one side, and her dark eyebrows raise a little in the middle, and those stupid fat lips of hers press together making the skin on her mouth wrinkle. There's nothing in the world like a look like that. Why the hell would she look at me out of pity. She's the one who should be getting the pity, and I'm the one who should be giving it as far as I'm concerned. She's the one who has the whole world figured out wrong from what I can tell. It's not me, lady.

In fact, I'm tired of thinking on it. I couldn't give a crap what they think about me anyways. But the windows in the office that look out into the hall, well, I wish those windows weren't there or had curtains on them or something to cover them the hell up. The last thing I need is my peers staring at me through the windows and laughing like something's so funny. They don't stand there long enough for me to see exactly who it is that feels the need to stare at my unfortunate luck. My eyes take some time to adjust and they're just too quick with their peeking for them to adjust. It's just like in the cafeteria with them flicking things to the back of my head. But I know there are a lot of them out there, and I know they are just staring right at me getting giddy as hell at how the tables have turned right back on me. It's making for a damn shame of a situation for me again. I should be used to it, but right now I can't stand it. Especially when I'm waiting in this uncomfortable chair to see the stupid school psychologist.

I know I'm supposed to be seeing the school psychologist because of my overhearing Mr. Robbins tell the office lady in a loud voice that I need to. He keeps saying, there's something wrong with his head, and that the school psychologist is who I need to see. It's not my head that's the problem though. I want to tell Mr. Robbins this, but right now I can tell is not the time. The timing of things is important in life. Mr. Robbins just keeps getting all worked up after every time the office lady shakes her head. I can't figure on how her tiny little head doesn't just snap off her neck every time she shakes it with all that banana-colored hair piled on top of her head. It must weigh a ton for chrissakes. So when I decide to listen to her, I hear her say that the stupid school psychologist is in the mountains. Right now I'd like to be in the mountains and out of this uncomfortable chair. I don't even know what the mountains are like considering I've never been there, but I know like there's no tomorrow that it has to be better than this chair.

But anyways, I get relieved when I hear I don't have to talk to the stupid school psychologist. I feel bad for Mr. Robbins though because of my knowing he's hot by now, super-hot as a matter of fact, and things get good and messed up when you're hot like that. He's not leaning in to talk to the office lady anymore, and it's looking like that breathing problem is coming back. I know he just wants me off his hands so he can get back to things being the way they are in his world and get the hell home to sweet little Mrs. Robbins.

All of a sudden, I hear the office lady call to the principal's office, and I can tell she does it just to get Mr. Robbins to shut the hell up. You can always tell when somebody does something just to shut somebody else the hell up. It's so obvious. She should brush up on her office lady skills if she wants to keep being the office lady around here. She tells the principal that there's things to be attended to out in the waiting area. She hangs the phone back up, squints her face at Mr. Robbins like he should be kissing her feet for doing something that's a part of her job anyhow, and then starts writing something down on a notepad in front of her that she suddenly found is so important. She won't even look at Mr. Robbins anymore. It's like he's not even there for chrissakes. It makes you feel bad for the guy. I'm telling you, anybody who wears those cheap press-on nails, especially the pink ones, are going to give you the time they want to give you and nothing more. It's just the unfortunate crappy way of things.

CHAPTER TWENTY-TWO

I'm tired of the crap that's going on here, so I find my own damn way into the principal's office. I don't want to see one more minute of the office lady ignoring Mr. Robbins right to his face. And besides that, I want to avoid the office lady myself considering it would be such a hassle for her to walk the hell around the counter and show me in. I know she told the principal to come into the waiting area, I heard it with my own two ears, but I'm not ashamed of what I did so I don't wait for the principal to come to me, I go to him. I'm not even going to mention how it's kind of a relief anyhow considering how I just want to be away from my peers and all their looking and laughing. I wish like there's no tomorrow things had gone my way. I'd be laughing all the way home by now if they had.

I walk the short way down the hall and open the door that says PRINCIPAL right across the front of it. It's all in caps just like that. I open it wide just to make sure it works considering I know how it must be closed all the time. You can't be principal of the whole damn place and have everybody always peeking their head into your business when you're trying hard to work. Things would never get done. So I look in after I open the door and the principal is just sitting at his desk with a pen in his hand writing something that looks important. It's a good thing I took things into my own hands and came in here because of it looks like he wasn't going to get the hell up out of his desk anytime soon. What is it with people around here anyhow. Mr. Robbins seems to be the only one in this whole place who knows a bad situation and takes it the hell seriously.

The principal doesn't even see me when I open his door. He doesn't hear me either for that matter. So I close the door behind me, not loud just normal, and sit down in a chair right across from him. It's a nice chair, too, with some padding and a place to rest my arms. Well, a place where I could rest my arms, but I don't all because of my keeping my hands deep in my coat pockets. It's just out of habit this time around, keeping my hands in my coat pockets. This is the kind of chair I don't mind taking a load off in and waiting a while until somebody has some time to deal with things. And right now that somebody happens to be the school principal.

His name is Principal Dr. Hathaway. Right away, even before he really takes the time to look up from what he's doing and look at me in the face, Principal Dr. Hathaway tells me, take off your coat. You know in that annoying voice people use when they tell you to take your coat off. At least he didn't add the, and stay a while, part. It gets good and under my skin when people add that. It's always in that annoying voice, too. But let me tell you something, I don't take it off considering you don't do things like take your coat off just because somebody like Principal Dr. Hathaway tells you to. I keep it zipped to the top and keep my hands shoved in my pockets and don't move a measly muscle.

Principal Dr. Hathaway is a big fat man, like a balloon that has way too much air in it and you think it's going to bust at any minute. You know the kind of fat I'm talking about. His fingers are so big they look like plump ready-to-cook-and-eat bratwursts. I don't know how he gets that fancy gold ring from that fancy college on his finger. When I was a kid Mom used to make those ready-to-cook-and-eat bratwursts every Saturday night. She doesn't do it anymore considering how I'm not a kid and how she's working the night shift every night of the week and how she doesn't have the time to cook much of anything tasty. But she used to make the bratwursts good. She'd boil them right in a pot of beer. I don't know how she came up with that idea, but it was tasty. Like I said before though, that was when I was a kid. I haven't had a tasty thing like that in forever. I'd give just about anything for a bratwurst right about now.

But right now, Principal Dr. Hathaway wants me to think on something else. It's obvious considering he keeps calling my name across his desk like I'm a stupid dog or something. He put his pen down a while ago, and now all his attention is good and on me. I'm not much listening to him so I can't blame him for keeping on calling my name out. Nobody wants somebody they are talking right at to not even pay them one little bit of attention, but on the other hand, nobody wants somebody to call their name out like a stupid dog either. So I tell him to stop calling my name out like that, and he does. People say Principal Dr. Hathaway is a plain bastard, but right now, I think what he just did was a stand-up thing to do. You know, to stop calling my name out like a stupid dog when I asked him to.

Anyways, he looks at me for a while. He's not saying a word, he's just looking at me. He folds his fat fingers together, but he can only get them to fold to his first knuckles. I'm thinking things like that must weigh on his mind good. You don't think on your fingers a whole lot if they're normal like most everybody's are normal. But if they're not and they're super-big, you couldn't help but think on them good and hard all the time. Right now though, he's not looking hard at his fingers, he's looking right smack-dab at me.

His looking doesn't bother me a bit. I just wish he had some food in that desk of his that he could give me while he's doing it. I'm hungry, and it's starting to get at me again. My stomach keeps clenching, and I can't hardly stand it. It would make things a lot easier if he even had a cracker in his drawer that he could give me. Sitting here wouldn't be so bad if I had some food in my stomach. I could just sit here all day long if that was the case.

Then all of a sudden, just like if you sneeze your brains out or something, the office lady comes in Principal Dr. Hathaway's office to bring him a tall glass of water that she sets on his desk. And then, just like that, almost in the same second, she drops my gun right next to his water. Just like that. With a loud crash it wakes everything the hell up. She just drops it on his desk. Where is that senseless lady's respect. It's a thing of beauty. You don't just drop a thing of beauty like that on a desk right in front of Principal Dr. Hathaway's bratwurst fingers.

Goddamnit. What the hell does she think she's doing. My prospects have already been ruined, and she and her cheap press-on fingernails feel the need to shove my face in it. And on top of that, she does it right in front of Principal Dr. Hathaway. I want to scream at her and tell her to go to hell, but I need to keep my cool and not show my emotions because of my already being in some serious trouble. I'm hot again and want to take that glass of water sitting on Principal Dr. Hathaway's desk and drink it down fast. But I think better of things before they get way out of hand. I'm no fool about things, and right now if I was to go for that water like I want to like nobody's business, the office lady and Principal Dr. Hathaway would think I was making for the gun. So I think better of things and just live with my being hot and my being disgusted with the office lady.

I'm expecting the office lady to leave after she comes in and does her office lady things. But instead she plants herself right behind Principal Dr. Hathaway and doesn't leave like any good office lady would know to do. She's just standing there with her hand on Principal Dr. Hathaway's shoulder. To make matters worse, she decides to open her big mouth. She tells me, you don't look so hot, and, you should at least wipe your face off before trying to sit here and talk to Principal Dr. Hathaway. What I want to say is, I know I don't look so hot lady and besides that I could really give a goddamn about it. But I don't considering that that would be exactly what she'd want me to do. I just stare her down until that big smile she has leaves her stupid face. Besides, it seems that they have me by the short and curlies anyways, so not much of what I would say is going to make a damn bit of difference. It's important to know your limits in life and know about people like the office lady.

Principal Dr. Hathaway asks me, why didn't your father teach you better than to bring something like that to school, while he points right at my gun with his bratwurst finger. I don't look at him in the face because of it being hard for me to lie when it's smack-dab right to somebody's face. So I look just over his thick shoulder that looks like it might bust out of his blue suit coat. The office lady still has her hand right there on his shoulder like she owns him or something, but I'm not looking at her stupid hand right now. I'm looking over his shoulder at the American flag folded into a triangle with all sorts of pins stuck in it.

I shrug to answer his question because of my knowing he didn't really want me to open my dumb mouth anyways. It's one of those, I'm-going-to-ask-you-a-question-because-I-want-to-hear-myself-talk, kinds of questions. Plus, I'm not going to answer any questions of any kind while the office lady is still standing around like she deserves to hear what I have to say for myself. Besides that, how do you tell somebody like Principal Dr. Hathaway that your old man has never been around your stupid life. You don't. The last thing Principal Dr. Hathaway wants to talk on right now is that sissy crap about not having a dad around in your life ever. In fact, I'm making my own self sick just thinking on it.

All of a sudden, just like I blinked too long or something, my gun is nowhere to be found. I'm looking hard to find it, but like I said before, you look once and there it is and then one stupid minute later, just like that, just like you pissed yourself or something, poof, it's just nowhere. My head starts spinning, and I see little bursts of white in the all black I'm seeing. I blink my eyes hard to see anything except the light show that's going on right now. It's not doing too much to help, but it does a little so I can at least see what's in front of me.

Principal Dr. Hathaway keeps talking, and I know like there's no tomorrow that he thinks what he's saying is important. He'd be offended if I didn't perk my ass up and listen to every pointless word he's saying, especially the ones where spit comes flying out of his fat mouth. Who the hell spits when they talk for chrissakes. Anyways, it's hard to listen to somebody when your gun that was right smack-dab in front of your face is now gone. I'm trying hard to figure on its whereabouts, and my mind's a blank.

I calm myself down quick though and I'm glad. The office lady leaves the room again. Thank God for that. Her cheap stupid perfume was starting to give me a headache. It made my eyes blurry and itch like hell. Not so blurry or itchy that I can't see Principal Dr. Hathaway though. He's still staring me down good and solid. He doesn't seem to miss that the office lady is gone. His face is the same as when I first walked in. I wish she would see it, too, so she'd know she doesn't mean as much as she thinks she does.

You have to respect a guy who can stare you down good like that. He's looking for a good long time and finally says, tell me in your own words what happened today. I hate it when somebody says that to you. Tell me in your own words. Whose words does he think I'm going to use. The Pope's for chrissakes. I'm not going to do any talking, but that would make Mom proud if I did use the Pope's words. She sure would get a kick out of it. She'd love to brag to the jokers at the shop that her son is an act of God, talking like the Pope. I'll never get the things Mom gets a kick out of.

But I start thinking, in my own words, of course, about what Principal Dr. Hathaway just asked me. He's still looking at me solid, so I think for about half a second of telling him. Some things though, they're just not meant to be heard by people like Principal Dr. Hathaway. Really, who's to say he wouldn't know what it is I'm talking about. I know he held a gun in his hand, and might've even pulled the trigger with his bratwurst fingers before. He told us all about how he was in Vietnam when he gathered the whole school up in the gym and told us all about it. But I still get this clear feeling, good and obvious, that Principal Dr. Hathaway wouldn't get it even if I explained the prospects to him in a simple fashion. You can't blame the guy, though. Most times, I bet he has enough to think on with all his fat and health and being afraid of dropping dead at any minute because his heart can't take it anymore.

He breaks my concentration by saying, well, to my face. Like that's supposed to make me talk or something. Just like that he says, well. Poor bastard. There are just some things he'll never understand. So I take my shoes off. Just by flicking off the heel with my other foot. It comes off easy. Now I just need to sit back and wait for the magic to happen like I know it will. Nobody, I don't care who you are, can stand the smell that comes when I take my shoes off. It can fill up your nose good, and you can't just sit there and take it. Me, well, I can stand it with them being my feet. You get good and used to those kinds of things over the years. So I sit here and keep my mouth shut. There's one thing I learned from Mom, and that's to keep your stupid mouth shut in these situations.

CHAPTER TWENTY-THREE

Anyways, the shoe trick worked well with Principal Dr. Hathaway like I knew it would. They smell good and like that fried cabbage that Mom tries to make and pass off for a meal is growing between my toes today. Principal Dr. Hathaway stood it for a lot longer than most people do when I take my shoes off, but nobody, I don't care who you are, can ignore it even if they try to. It's a thing of beauty when things play out just he way you have them in your head. He gave it his all, but in the end, he sent me packing, smelly feet and all, back to the front of the office where I was before I sat down for my heart-to-heart with Principal Dr. Hathaway.

The only problem is that now I have to sit back down on the same hard stupid chair I sat on like I told you about before, so maybe getting out of Principal Dr. Hathaway's office wasn't such a good thing after all. Sure, I don't have to sit there while Principal Dr. Hathaway fires questions at me that I'm not going to answer, but now I'm stuck again with the office lady and the windows where my peers can stare at me like I'm a monkey at the zoo. Let me tell you something, I'm not a monkey at the zoo that they can just watch because they paid their two dollars. But nobody's telling them to get the hell back from the window, so nothing's really stopping them from doing whatever the hell it is they want to. I guess that's pretty typical around this place though. Goddamn typical.

Aren't they supposed to be in class by now. I know they have other places to be other than standing right outside the office looking in. I want to flip them off or something, you know give them a good long bird, but I don't. I shove my hand further in my coat pockets to make sure I don't. You have to keep your head about you and not give them what they want like they actually did pay two dollars to see what they want to see. I'm glad I keep my cool. It's not easy, but I do good considering.

I look around for Mr. Robbins, but he's nowhere the hell around. I just knew it. He wanted me off his hands quick. I'll bet he shot out of here like a bat out of hell just as soon as I went into Principal Dr. Hathaway's office and shut the door behind me. A part of me keeps looking to see if he's going to come back into the office at any minute to see things through, but the other part of me is too smart to fall for it. In fact, Mr. Robbins probably didn't even make it to his afternoon classes. He probably went home to get cleaned up and get into a new green button-down sweater. Nobody wants to walk around with somebody else's puke all down the front of them. I get that. But the one part of me that's thinking he's going to come back is hard to shut the hell up. It's not like Mr. Robbins to leave me hanging like he is right now like I'm a rotten pair of panties hanging on a laundry line.

I know Mr. Robbins, and I know that he can sometimes know the way of things pretty good. Like this one time I turned in an assignment that was supposed to be about our favorite person in history who has meant something to our life. I couldn't stand to give one thought to the assignment or to people who have been dead for a long time. What good are they to me anyways. Who the hell cares about what somebody did forever ago before things came to be the way they are, so I didn't pick somebody from actual history. I wrote about my so-called dad who's never bothered to show his stupid mug around my life. Let me tell you something, he's meant a whole lot of wasteful things to my life, and I've never even met the bastard. Well, not until today that is. I found out all about what a pansy he really is today.

Anyways, Mr. Robbins said once at the very beginning of school that he didn't care how we turned in our homework. He said he didn't care if it was in pen or pencil or how messy it was, he just wanted us, my so-called peers and myself, to turn something the hell in. For some reason it stuck with me. So I took what Mr. Robbins said to heart when it came to the assignment I'm telling you about. I decided I'd go into the drawer in Mom's room where she keeps her underwear and lipstick and other things she finds important, and grab a maxi pad that she uses when she's busy losing babies and the other thing once a month, you know bleeding from where it is that women bleed from. I don't know what made me do it, I just did it. So I get the maxi pad, bring it into my room, shut the door, and write about the bastard right there on the maxi pad. I knew Mom would probably get good and on my case for taking the thing because of those kinds of things being expensive. She'd also say how I do nothing but waste her slutty money on doing stupid things like writing a report right there smack-dab in the middle of her maxi pad. But I didn't really give a crap considering I was pleased with my good idea on how to try out Mr. Robbins. I was willing to deal with Mom if it came down to it.

You can't write too much on a maxi pad, so my report wasn't long. Not that I had a whole lot to say on the bastard anyhow, or that I wanted to write the thing in the first place, but I wrote it considering how much I thought Mr. Robbins was a stand-up guy. I printed my name across the top in clear letters to avoid confusion as to whose report it was that was being turned in on a maxi pad. I made it clear, DUSTY SPARROW, in all caps just like that, too. There was no mistaking it. I got a D on it because of my not following the assignment. I expected it. But Mr. Robbins didn't get on my case, he didn't ride me at all. Not one little bit. Most teachers would have kicked me out of class right then when I handed the thing in, and they would've done it fast for handing in a report written smack-dab in the middle of a maxi pad. Mr. Robbins though, he's that kind of stand-up guy.

I thought the maxi pad thing would have gotten a rise out of him, but this, I didn't really expect that he wouldn't follow this one through. I at least thought he'd stick around to see how everything turned out. That's why the half of me keeps looking the hell around waiting for him to pop his mug into things again. I thought we had a thing going, the two of us. I thought he understood the things behind the things I do. I guess I was wrong on that one like I've been wrong on a lot of things today. But like I said before, as crappy as it is to say, things about Mr. Robbins are going down fast in my head.

I finally make myself realize that Mr. Robbins isn't going to come back no matter how my head keeps telling me he will. I'm stuck in this hard-ass chair all on my own. I turn my head to my left and notice the walls for the first time. I don't even want to mention the color they painted the walls in here. When you're in a position like I am right at this moment, it's the last color you want to deal with. It's a light blue color. Not super-light, but like the color of the sky on a clear day when there's not one cloud around to screw things up. It's like the color of a room for a brand new baby that just came into things. I would like it on a usual day, but today it gets me annoyed like I want to spit on it. I want to get a big fat luggie in my mouth and spit it good and hard right on the wall with a big ass splat. But I hold back for reasons that aren't super-clear to me. I guess it could be because of my knowing it's not the time or the place to act on your impulses anymore. Things could get good and ugly if I did.

And right now not only is the chair uncomfortable to sit in and the walls are enough to take your head places you don't want it to go, but the place smells like bandages. I didn't notice it before, but I'm smelling it now like nobody's business. I know the smell of bandages good because of when I was close with Dave Treadway I smelled them all the time. I don't remember a day when Dave didn't have a bandage across his forearm or chin. I'd ask him why it was that he was always wearing a bandage. He never had a good answer. I know when somebody's business is their business though and Dave and the bandages, well, they were his business so I didn't press him on the subject. I'll never forget that smell, so as I'm sitting here right now I know like there's no tomorrow that that's what that smell is. I'm starting not to like it as much the longer it is that I sit here though. I don't want to think on Dave Treadway right at the moment either considering he'd know just how I took a good thing with the prospects and blew it right out of the water. I'm kicking myself good and hard all on my own. The last thing I'd need right now is Dave Treadway saying, way to fuck things up Dusty old boy.

I hear somebody talking to me so I stop thinking about the stupid bandages. It's Miss Office Lady and she's saying, we're going to have to call your mom. She doesn't say she is going to call Mom, she says they are going to call Mom like she doesn't have enough balls to take responsibility for something she's about to do. She keeps looking at me like I should say something so I say, don't bother. But I know she's going to no matter how much I'm telling her the truth. She tells me to be quiet because of her thinking that anything I have to say isn't worth a damn. Not that she has too much reason to listen to me without the gun, I'm no fool you know, but it doesn't mean that I don't give a crap about things. It's the nasty kick of things when you want to say something and nobody'll listen because of somebody else having the gun instead of me. Who has it by now is something I'm not too sure on, but I know it sure as hell isn't me.

What the hell good is Mom anyways. I know she's asleep and she'll be mad when the phone wakes her up. It's going to be good and ugly. I can just see her now in my head. It's the same old thing. Mom says that she likes to keep people on their toes being unpredictable, but let me tell you something, I can tell you whatever the hell she is doing at any time of the day. She probably got that word from one of those books she's never even read before. I know like there's no tomorrow Mom thinks she's unpredictable, but that's just not the way of things. I know that office lady is going to get into some things when Mom picks up the phone that I know she has to get the hell up off the couch to get. The last thing you want to do is get Mom the hell up off the couch. I was just trying to help the lady out. People should realize when it is that you're just trying to help them out.

The office lady looks on some card that must have my phone number on it and dials the phone with the tip of the press-on nail on her right pointer finger. She's holding all of her other fingers straight out to make good and sure the rest of them don't touch any part of the phone. It's always about those press-on nails whenever it is that somebody has them on the end of their finger. She waits for a minute holding the phone to her ear. I can tell it starts ringing because of the lady putting the phone between her ear and shoulder to wait. She needs to free up her hands to keep them from getting worked too much.

For a minute, I think Mom isn't even going to answer the phone because of the office lady starts digging into her scalp with one of her cheap pink press-on nails. I know the phone is just ringing and ringing. And ringing for chrissakes. But the office lady doesn't hang up like most people would. Most people get irritated listening to all that ringing right in their ear. It gets good and under my skin, and I'm not even on the phone. So all of a sudden, I hear the office lady talking into the phone with that office-lady voice that I know isn't even her real voice. She makes it stuffy like she's so damn important. It's almost like she's talking through her nose instead of her mouth. I know that's going to be the first thing that gets to Mom. The last thing she can stand is when somebody calls on the phone and acts like they are more important than they are. Like they own the whole world or something.

I know Mom is rubbing the back of her neck, like she always does, to get the crick out of her neck while listening to whatever the hell it is the office lady is blabbing into her ear. She's always rubbing the crick out when she gets up off the couch because of there being no pillows to put her head on. Things get uncomfortable when you don't have pillows. I know the office lady is thinking to herself that she can charm the ugly right out of Mom if she talks long enough and says things like darlin' and sweetie in that office-lady voice she thinks she's perfected. I know she's thinking that Mom is like most moms around this place. The kind of mom who really gives a goddamn about their kid and who would freak the hell out when their kid gets a crooked hair up their ass acting on their instincts, which isn't the way they were raised to act.

    I can tell by her face that the things she thought were true in this life have all been shot to hell with one phone call to Mom. It didn't take long. This might be a record, even for Mom. It makes me feel a little bad for the office lady because of my knowing how Mom can crap things up in your head once she's in there, but I tried to tell her so I can't feel all the way bad. If she would have just listened to me and think I might actually know what it is that I'm saying when it comes to Mom instead of looking at me like I have three heads or something, she'd still be happy in her situation and not turned flat the hell on her back like she is now.

    All of a sudden, just like one of her nails popped off or something, the office lady turns red. She's the color of a tasty shiny ripe apple by now. What I wouldn't give for a tasty apple right now. It might help things along for me. I hear her say, I understand thank you, and then just hangs up the phone. Just like that she hangs up the phone with no goodbye or anything. The way people act sometimes, well, I can't figure it out. I don't talk on the phone much, well, practically never, but even I know you say goodbye before you hang the thing up. These are the things I've been telling you about people. The way they act is a simple disgrace. Sometimes it's a damn shame.

    It's funny how she doesn't have anything so smart to say about my appearance now, does she. In fact, she won't even look at me. She doesn't say anything clever like, you should at least wipe your face off before you sit in this office. I almost want to say something right to her face like, did a cat get your tongue now all of a sudden Miss Fat-Lipped Banana-Colored Hair Pink Press-On Nails No-Manners Office Lady. But I don't, because of my not being a nasty bastard. I'd like to though bad, but I've been on the other end of that line with Mom too many times to count. I know how she's feeling right now like a tiny little ant Mom just flung off her shoulder. You can't feel any lower than when Mom is done with you. Well, I guess you can feel lower, you can always feel worse about things, but you sure as hell don't want to. Nobody, not even the annoying office lady, deserves what Mom thinks they deserve. So I decide to keep my opinions to myself because of it being the wrong time and the wrong place.

I don't know what the hell it is that Mom said to her on the phone, but I can make a pretty good guess. After she hangs up the phone, she won't even look at me sideways, much less tell me whatever the hell it was that Mom did say. She just grabs her big purse from behind the counter where she must stash it in case of emergencies like this one and pulls out her face powder makeup and dabs it on her nose and neck. I've never seen anybody put face powder makeup on their neck before, but then again I've never seen a lot of things. Still, it doesn't make much sense to me. But she closes the thing and puts it back into her big purse back under the counter and starts picking off her fake pink press-on nails. One by one and she doesn't stop till she's got the whole lot of them in a pile in front of her.

Whatever Mom must've said must've been good and rotten. I've seen lots of strange things when it comes to Mom though, so I'm not even going to guess at it. I said very plain and clear not to call Mom. I know the things she can do. I don't know what she thought I meant when I said it. I bet she does now though and wishes like hell she would've listened to what I was saying. These are the kinds of things I'm talking about. I'm not just talking out of my ass, Miss Office Lady.

CHAPTER TWENTY-FOUR

Leave it to Mom to send Mike the sonofabitch to pick me up. Just when I think things are as bad as they're going to get, I have to deal with that guy. Who wants to see a crappy sonofabitch like him on the streets much less know the guy and have to have him come pick you up from school. Mom knows I think he's a sonofabitch, and she sends him anyways. I can already hear her excuses. She always has good ones on hand when things go to hell like this situation here. I know this time she'll play like she couldn't come because of her having no car, and that she sends Mike the sonofabitch because he has a car. Never mind that it's crappy, it's still a car. I know the sonofabitch Mike does it considering he's caught a thing for Mom just like all the other jokers. Everybody catches a thing when it comes to Mom, but his seems to be the worst I've ever seen. That guy'll do anything for her. Anything at all.

As soon as I see Mike the sonofabitch, I wish like hell that it wasn't him who showed up. But there isn't anything that guy wouldn't do when it comes to Mom like I was telling you about before. If I was him, I would've told her to use some of her slutty money to get her own goddamn car and take care of her own goddamn kid. Things just don't seem to work out that way when it comes to anything involving anything with Mom though. I'm surprised sometimes that she even has to get up off the couch to do anything with Mike the sonofabitch around to do whatever the hell it is she asks for. It's disgusting.

As soon as I see Mike the sonofabitch, I get a funny thought in my head, a weird one I don't know where the hell it came from. I start thinking on that short bastard. You know, my so-called dad. That smartie. I have a thing against smarties, especially that short bastard. But now I'm thinking like there's no tomorrow I'd rather that short bastard walked through the door instead of the sonofabitch Mike, you know, taking responsibilities for his mix-ups even if it is a lot of years too late. Life is full of mix-ups, and I take all kinds of responsibility for my own. Like right now, I'm taking responsibility for my being dumb and losing my cool with that stupid Brian Farrell. I'm not even going to mention Candy Carmichael because of my needing to keep it cool now. We don't need another mix-up to add to the list right at the moment. I've already done a pretty good job at ruining all the prospects I had right in my hot stupid hand. I'm kicking myself good for that one. If that short bastard showed up, I'd be more likely to not get mad at things in an already bad situation. At least I'd know that he was here without it having anything to do with Mom and the way she is. It's plain that he doesn't even remember her. But that's Mom for you, always getting the last word in even when she's nowhere the hell around.

So I see Mike the sonofabitch standing there trying to talk to the office lady playing like he's an upstanding citizen. He starts his sentences with stand-up kinds of words like he knows what they mean instead of the cuss bombs like he's used to using. Now there's a guy who you'd expect to hear all kinds of filth coming out of his cheap mouth. Everybody knows he's a sonofabitch though. Even the office lady. You can just tell by her face. Her eyes are looking at him, but I know they aren't taking the time to understand the guy. Nobody that likes somebody looks at them with a face like that.

He's only there for a minute though whispering something right to her that only she can hear before she touches her big banana-colored hair and smiles all big because she can't help it. She's blushing by now good and rosy, and then scoops up her fake press-on nails that she pulled off out of the madness that she caught from Mom so Mike the sonofabitch won't get some sort of wrong impression. Like since her fake press-on nails were on the counter instead of on her fingertips, she's not worth a damn. Who gives a crap what kind of an impression that sonofabitch gets. I guess there's just things that are important to people like the office lady. They're the kinds of things Mike the sonofabitch knows how to get at in a half a second. He can smell them a mile away.

They talk for a while longer all hushed like they are the only two people around in the whole world. Then I see the office lady get something out from under the counter where she stashes her purse. I can't see what it is, but I see her slide it across the counter to Mike the sonofabitch. I'm thinking it's her face powder makeup. But why would she give him her face powder makeup. There's been stranger things that have happened, so I don't give it too much of my thinking.

I see Mike the sonofabitch turn around and look at me in that how-could-you-do-this-to-your-mother kind of way. It's amazing how he can switch gears like that all in a half a second. I want to tell him bad that he and the office lady and the rest of the world can all get on the first train to hell, but before I can even get the words to the tip of my tongue, I stop. The sonofabitch is still looking right into my face, but my attention gets caught by what he's holding in his hand. It's one of those sandwich baggies, well, a little bigger than your normal sandwich baggie, that I see some of my so-called peers take tasty looking sandwiches out of sometimes at lunch. But it's not a tasty sandwich in the baggie, and it's clearly not the face powder makeup I thought it might be either. I can see that plain as day. It's a rusty lead pipe that looks from here like it's about the same size as my hand. My hands are pretty big, and I bet that thing goes from the bottom of my palm to the tip of my middle finger.

What the hell is Mike the sonofabitch doing with a lead pipe in a sandwich baggie for chrissakes. And on top of that, why the hell did Miss Office Lady give it to him. I squint my eyes hard to see what it is that's on the outside of the sandwich baggie. My eyes aren't so good like I told you about before, so it takes them a while to get adjusted to the squinting. What comes into focus after a minute is a big piece of masking tape. I know it's masking tape because of my having to put it on the floor behind the register at the shop to mark where it was I had to sit myself while I was there considering having a kid there would be bad for business. But it's masking tape plain as day with my name printed across it in all caps. DUSTY SPARROW. I hate the way it looks written down as much as I hate my name. It says it just like that in the stupid office lady's bubbly handwriting. I know it's her handwriting, there's no mistaking it. It looks just like her.

I'm confused as all hell as to what's going on. I look up again into Mike the sonofabitch's face. He's rolling his big fat tongue over his crooked teeth, and I feel my stomach fizz again like I'm going to blow just like I did all over Mr. Robbins's favorite green button-down sweater. Mike the sonofabitch opens his big mouth wide and says, see a ghost there Dusty boy. He says it and laughs out loud hard like there's no tomorrow. He's always thinking he's a funny guy. I hate his crooked teeth. I don't puke all over the place though, and I'm glad I don't. The janitors don't need to be cleaning up after me today. It's not an easy one to talk down, so it's taking me a few minutes to get back my composure. You need to realize when you're about to lose it, and you need to take the time to get it back before you move the hell on to something else.

Mike the sonofabitch is snapping his fingers at me. He's stopped his laughing by now, but he's calling my name out like I'm a stinking dog he wants to get out of his filthy trash. I'm not a dog, though, so I don't answer. He doesn't deserve one measly ounce of my breath. I know I'm going to have to go with Mike the sonofabitch, you can always tell when it is that your options have just played themselves out, but nobody says I have to make it easy. I can't hardly stand to look at Mike the sonofabitch sideways much less get in a car with him like I know I'm going to have to do. The last thing I want to do is get in that piece-of-crap car I know is going to be good and hot, but when you're out of choices like I am right at this minute, well, you're out of choices. That's it. Period.

I try one last ditch effort to think up any excuse not to go with him. I'm pretty much tapped as far as that goes though. He shakes the sandwich baggie in front of my face like it's supposed to mean something. Miss Office Lady seems like her patience is running way the hell out with the both of us. I know like there's no tomorrow she wishes we'd leave quick so she can dial up her pals from the bowling league I know she must belong to or something. I know it's irritating for her not to be able to call her stupid friends and talk her usual nonsense because of her being the last one stuck with me. It's the real bitch of things when you're the last one on the totem pole. Crap is always going down hill, and it stinks like hell. I know these things good.

Pretty soon the office lady gets fed up and says, you're free to go. She obviously means with Mike the sonofabitch. Like he's my stupid dad for chrissakes. I try to think up most anything because of my knowing if I go with Mike the sonofabitch, then I'm locked in. Throw away the key. I know like there's no tomorrow there's no getting back to the grocery store on the nice street today. I feel bad and rotten considering my promise to the lady with the butterfly coat. Things don't matter much if you can't have your word be your word. Most times I can think of excuses to get out of things like right now, but not today. Today I'm wore out.

Anyways, sometimes it's just easier to nod and go on even if it's the last thing on earth you want to do. My options are out, so I get up out of the hard uncomfortable chair that I finally got used to. It wouldn't be so bad to stay in that chair now with everything going the way it's going. Now the office lady can play with her banana-colored hair and call her stupid friends and actually have something worth a damn to say for once. Funny how everybody else is cashing in on my prospects, and I have to get in a crappy car with Mike the sonofabitch who's wearing the same gray pants as usual that smell like hell. Some people don't appreciate a good thing when it comes along. I would, but things just don't work out that way sometimes.

BVG